T0102059

THE BORDER IS BURNING

THE BORDER IS
BURNING

ITO ROMO

University of New Mexico Press ◊ Albuquerque

© 2013 by Ito Romo
All rights reserved. Published 2013
Printed in the United States of America

First paperback printing 2023 | ISBN 978-0-8263-6566-8

LIBRARY OF CONGRESS CATALOGING-IN-PUBLICATION DATA

Romo, Ito, 1961–
  The border is burning / Ito Romo.
    pages cm

  ISBN 978-0-8263-5334-4 (cloth : alk. paper) — ISBN 978-0-8263-5335-1 (electronic)
  1. Mexican-American Border Region—Fiction. 2. Mexican Americans—
Fiction. 3. Immigrants—United States—Fiction. 4. Mexico—Emigration and
immigration—Fiction. 5. Violence—Mexican-American Border Region—
Fiction. 6. Domestic fiction. I. Title.
  PS3568.O56546B67 2013
  813>.54—dc23

                    2013003771

With sincere appreciation to the Artist Foundation of San Antonio and The
Department of Culture and Creative Development from the City of San Antonio.

Cover art by Vincent Valdez
Cover design by Min Marcus
Design and composition by Lila Sanchez
Text composed in Arno Pro 10.75/14.5
Display type is Futura Std

To my mother, Minerva Villarreal Romo,
tree of a long line of South Texas Mesquite,
noble in the face of drought,
grace to leaf when winter's finally gone.

CONTENTS

BABY MONEY

M any, many years ago, when I was just thirteen years old, I saw the two-headed baby floating in its jar of formaldehyde at the carnival by the river, on the American side. I threw up. Right there and then, in the middle of the tent, in front of all my friends, as we listened to the man with the microphone barking the baby's sad story in his eerie voice. My friends all thought I threw up because we had just been on the Tilt-A-Whirl.

The water crawled over the banks of the Rio Grande into her home so suddenly that she had to hoist her two small children onto her shoulders and wade out of the rising water to higher ground. The children clapped and cheered for the tumultuous, growing river, the rain hitting their faces and soaking their old, torn T-shirts and shorts.

Soon the river was once again at their feet. She cried. Anger and jealousy raced through her veins. Bending down, she filled her cupped hand with river water and raised it to her forehead in the sign of the cross, letting some flow down onto her lips.

She asked the river to be kind to their home, grabbed the children by the hand, and began their way to her sister's cardboard house across town in the outskirts of Nuevo Laredo, right past the dreaded La Loma jail. The fact that the neighborhood was controlled by narcos only made it safer than if the cops could still go in there. She knew they could wait out the storm safely there.

～

I didn't eat well for days, and somehow I knew I would have that same feeling in the pit of my stomach for the rest of my life—a fear so intense it made me throw up.

The flood was the well-deserved wrath of God, I thought. The tail end of a tropical storm had swept through from the Gulf across the Rio Grande Valley, and it settled right above the sister cities, dumping fourteen inches of rain in less than twenty-four hours. The river swelled, and within minutes of the first heavy downpour, the river had overrun its banks, leaving the carnival in two or three feet of water—ponies, cotton candy, and all. The carnavaleros hadn't even had time to save the giant stuffed animals, which became bottom-heavy with water. Their bright colors ran into each other where they touched. And in the midst of the deluge, the two-headed baby, which had been sitting in a jar of formaldehyde on a wobbly wooden table, floated away, out of the tent, into the Rio Grande.

～

After the floodwaters had receded, after the carnival people had had a chance to replace the carousel's twinkling light bulbs that had short-circuited and popped, after the giant, surrealistic portrait of the two-headed baby had been taken down, she walked back into her cardboard shantytown house by the river to dredge the mud out of her two small rooms and see what was left.

She screamed.

The two-headed baby, still in its giant mayonnaise jar, was half-buried in the muddy floor. She stared for a long time at the glass jar, tilted on its side in the mud, a ray of sunlight reflecting off the rounded top.

"Gringos bárbaros," she said softly, knowing about the reward in the Mexican newspaper. She wiped the mud from the heavy glass jar with the hem of her old, black skirt, and cradled the jar awkwardly in her arms.

She placed the baby on the rusty folding bed she and her children shared with her husband, a drunk who worked in the oil fields of Veracruz, and who only came home once a year at Christmas. She was up to her ankles in mud—a big, bamboo tree trunk had gotten jammed in her door, a bright pink plastic grocery bag caught on one end.

She rolled up her sleeves, pulled up her skirt, tucked it in at the waist, and began clearing the mud off the simple square of bricks that formed their hearth so she could light a fire to dry the place out. As she scraped the last bits of mud from the top of the bricks with a piece of river stick, she thought about what she could get for her children with the five-hundred-American-dollar reward— a clean, safe apartment, small, but clean and safe—the medicines for the little one's asthma—the shoes they so badly needed—a nice meal of cabrito and frijoles borachos at La Principal for everyone. In a rage, she got up and ran to the edge of the river, yelling across to the American side, "I don't want your dammit baby money," over and over again, until she stood there in a daze, hyperventilating in the hot sun and the humidity.

She walked back into the house, staring at the wet ground below her, mesmerized by the sun's bright light shining on the sandy bank. She knelt again in front of the hearth and began removing the bricks, one by one, stacking them to the side. She was covered in sweat. The clouds had cleared, and the sun, now shining brightly again, hit the tin roof and turned the hut into a steamy oven. She looked around the room for something to dig with. She found nothing, so she opened her tiny cupboard and grabbed a tin plate to use as a shovel. Back at the hearth, she started digging like a madwoman. She dug deep. In fact, she dug so deep that she had to lie flat on the mud, the hole in front of her, her arms barely able to reach the bottom to scrape out still more dirt. She got up and looked around for the plastic flowers she had found in a broken vase in the dumpster by the bridge a long time ago. She knew they were around somewhere. Unless, of course, the river had washed them away when it had turned over the little wooden table that the broken vase and flowers had been sitting on. Bending down, she finally spotted them under the cupboard. She reached for them and sat down cross-legged on the mud. There she wove the plastic flowers into a crown.

She got up and balanced the heavy jar, holding the baby upright on the wet bed, then reached down to the floor for the flower crown. She placed it around the lid of the jar and fastened it by tightening the wire. She stared at the baby for a while, then she took the jar gently, set it down into the hole where she laid the baby to bed. Then she walked out to the river's edge with a cup in her hand, filled it with water, and walked back into the house, holding a dark, heavy riverbed rock in her other hand. Placing the cup of water by the hole, she lay down on the muddy floor again.

She struck the jar once, and it broke exactly in half.

The shock of formaldehyde struck her face.

She fainted.

～

A photo of the baby in the glass jar appeared in the newspaper a day later, in the back pages, next to Hints from Heloise and Your Daily Horoscopes. Underneath the picture, it read, $500 REWARD FOR THE RETURN OF THE TWO-HEADED BABY.

When I saw it, I ran to the bathroom and threw up.

～

When she woke up, weak and pensive, she stared at the child in the broken jar for a long time. Finally, she reached down into the hole again and pulled the bottom half of the jar from under the baby's feet and slipped the top half off over the baby's heads. She placed the jar next to the baby, sharp edges pushed into the soft ground so as not to hurt it, and placed the plastic flowers over the baby's heads like a crown. She sprinkled river water from the cup into the grave "en el nombre del Padre, del Hijo, y del Espíritu Santo." Still waking, she filled the grave with damp dirt, laid the bricks back in place, and covered them up with mud.

～

On the next day, my Tía Lalis and I stood on the bridge while the water flowed under us just a couple of feet away from the rails. The ragged kids selling newspapers, dry mud caking their shoes, wailed out the news of the reward for the two-headed baby. One of them stuck a copy of the paper in my face. There he was again, in living color, on the front page. I grabbed on to the bridge's rail, stood on the very tip of my toes, and locked my chin on the railing, my head over the side. I threw up again into the waters of the Rio Grande.

CHICKEN POT PIE

Will Ramirez looked in the rearview mirror to the backseat, eyes focused, opened wide, and scolded the two of his three boys that were sitting in the back. "Eat the damn chicken pot pie, for Christ's sake."

They were complaining about the food. He'd gotten the pies for them at the truck stop at the exit to Artesia Wells. Zapped the pot pies in the micro. He seat-belted the kids back into their seats, two in the back, one in front with him—cold Mountain Dew between their knees, a warm pie in each lap, white plastic spoon stuck into each pie—and got back on the highway.

"But, Dad, it looks like vomit," Memo said from the backseat. That's what had brought on the scolding.

The pies were cheap, though, and Will Ramirez was determined to save money, especially on food, since the kids would get a late supper at their grandmother's house in Laredo. His ex-wife's mother. He had offered to drive them down there; she was stuck in a seasonal job, gift-wrapping at the Dillard's in the mall down-town. Although the drive was not that long—just 154 miles—gas was expensive. He saved wherever he could. Three kids and an ex-wife cost a lot. He never had any money left.

He loved the boys, though, loved them in his own way—ma-cho, hard. They were boys after all, not little sissies.

It was dark already. They still had about an hour to go. But the kids said they were hungry, so he stopped.

At the Truck Mart, Memo, the oldest, had said, "We want pizza. There's a Pizza Hut across the street, Dad." He pointed out the huge glass window.

"No, corn dogs, Dad," Tony, the one in the middle, had said.

"No, Dad, McDonald's. We want a McDonald's. McDonald's. Dad, McDonald's." This was René, the little one.

"The pot pies are better for you. They have vegetables. I'm gonna get them, and you're gonna eat them," he had said. "Better than no damn hot dog. And a hell of a lot cheaper than McDonald's or Pizza Hut."

"Dad!" they had all yelled together.

"Be quiet. Go wait in the car. Memo, take them to the car. Roll down the windows a little. I'll be there in two minutes."

When he stopped yelling at the kids in the backseat, he looked at René, who was sitting up front with him, to see how *he* was doing with *his* chicken pot pie. The kid's eyes were teary.

"What's wrong with you?" he asked. The kid wasn't eating. "Why are you messing with your food? Do I have to get mad at you, too? Eat the damn food, René."

Will returned his gaze to the road, angry, biting his lower lip.

The little one threw up the four spoonfuls of chicken pot pie he had force-swallowed. They went right back into the pie tin. He turned to look at his father, maybe to tell him what had just hap-pened. But nothing came out. He just stared.

"Eat the damn chicken pot pie, René!" he yelled without turning. Then, looking into the rearview mirror, "Eat it all now, all of you. Finish it all, or I'll turn right back around and go back to San Antonio, no damn Christmas vacation for you. We'll go back home and take you back to your mamma's house. You guys hear me? I'm tired. Worked hard all damn day long just to hand the damn check over to your mother. Now eat your food. You hear me?"

"Yes."

The radio got snowy. Will pushed in a cassette that was popped halfway out of the player.

René was terrified because he knew he had to finish the chicken pot pie. Or no Christmas. And he planned for Christmas at his grandmother's all year. His grandmother set up a Nativity scene every year in her living room with about five hundred miniature figurines in it, and she never said no to him when he asked if he could "put something on there, Wela," no matter how "stupid" it seemed to his older brothers. The very first Christmas that he could remember at his grandmother's he had added a dinosaur he'd gotten in a box of cereal during the movie *Jurassic Park*. So for the last three years, he'd search for months and months before Christmas for the perfect toy, the perfect trinket to add to her Nativity scene. Last year he placed a giant plastic goldfish he'd traded from a kid in school after show-and-tell. It was made out of clear, squishy plastic that made the fish look particularly real, except for its size, of course. The giant goldfish hadn't fit into the foil river his grandma had molded to simulate the water cascading from one level to another, so she went into the kitchen and brought out a big piece of heavy-duty foil and molded it into a kidney-shaped lake and placed it at the end of the river on the lowest tier, as if the river emptied there. In it, she placed René's plastic fish and said, "See, m'ijito, it fits perfectly."

The huge scene had grown from one small corner to half the size of the living room in the fifty plus years his grandmother had been putting it up. This year, he'd begged his father to take him to McDonald's for his birthday lunch. Will, no matter what, made it a point to pick up all the boys for lunch whenever it was one of the kids' birthdays, even if it was during the week, on a school day. He'd get special permission to let them all out at the same time for lunch.

René didn't particularly like McDonald's; ketchup made him feel like throwing up, and Will refused to special order for any of his kids. "You should learn to eat your food like a man," he'd say. But the food wasn't the reason he'd wanted to go there. It was the plastic *Star Wars* figurine he saw advertised on TV, free with every kid's meal, that he was after—the Jabba the Hut. It was the only animal he could think of that she didn't have.

He swallowed slowly, spoon after spoon after spoon of thrown-up chicken pot pie until it was all gone. When he had finally finished and felt as if he'd throw up again, he reached to touch Jabba the Hut tucked away underneath his thigh. His stomach started to settle. Now he knew his dad would not turn around. Now he could go see his grandmother's nacimiento, and there they'd decide together exactly where among the clay figurines they'd place Jabba. Perhaps among the shepherds and their sheep, or with the farmers and their burros. Maybe with the women balancing trays of bread on their heads, or among the children carrying pails of water or small bundles of wheat on their backs toward the manger. A dreamlike land of sparkling lights and dried moss before him, a miniature universe of crushed paper grocery bags spray-painted to look like stone, darkened ceilings filled with a thousand silver stars dangling from invisible wire, tails of silver icicles, swinging across the sky like comets every time someone opened the living room door. Here, sitting in front of that Nativity scene, René realized what magic was.

After a while, Will looked again into the rearview mirror and asked, "You eat your food?"

"Yes," they answered.

"No, you haven't, Memo," said Tony. "Dad, he's lying."

"No, I'm not. Don't believe him, Dad. I'm almost finished. Look," Memo said. "Don't stop, Dad, don't stop. Look, last spoon." He shoved the last piece of crust and two tiny pieces of carrot and a pea into his mouth.

Will looked at René. He was crying. He felt like throwing up again.

"What's a matter with you now?"

"Nothing," he answered.

"Nothing? Then why are you crying, huh?"

"No reason."

"Then stop crying. If you have nothing to cry about, then don't cry. Stop crying, dammit. You know what, I have three little girls, don't I?"

The kids in the back started laughing.

"Muchachita," said Memo. "René is a muchachita."

"Yeah, mu-cha-chi-ta, mu-cha-chi-ta, mu-cha-chi-ta," chanted Tony.

"I'm not a muchachita," said René, turning, clicking open the seat belt to jump into the backseat, arms flailing, tears flying. "You're a bitch. The both of you. That's what you two are. A bitch."

Will reached over instantly, slapped the kid on the mouth hard with the back of his hand. Saliva flew into the back seat. Some landed on Memo's face. He didn't even dare move to wipe it off.

René sat back in place. He was bleeding. Tender, tiny lip cut. He didn't say a word. Just looked ahead over the dashboard to the stars in the sky, thought about his Wela, cried silently.

Will wrung the steering wheel's rubber cover. He knew what

he'd done. Lost control. Just lost control. He flipped on the cabin light. Saw the blood.

He reached into his back pocket, pulled out his handkerchief, and handed it to the kid. Turned the light off. Stared at the road in front of them.

A huge whitetail jumped out into the middle of the road and froze.

"Dad!" yelled one of the kids from the backseat.

"Watch it, Dad!" yelled the other.

They barreled right into it. The windshield exploded. Will's eyes filled with shattered glass, then blood and coarse deer hair. He could see nothing, just a bright red glow—one of the head-lights had twisted on impact onto the crushed sheet metal of the hood. It was still lit, still wired, shining into the car. As tightly as he held on to the steering wheel, he still couldn't control the car. The two right wheels grabbed the edge of the road's shoulder like a track. The car must have hit a stone or a break in the asphalt or something because, suddenly, it flew off the shoulder into a shallow ditch that acted like a ramp and made the car flip, then roll over twice before landing back on its tires, smoking.

There was silence for a while. Then Will started to hear cars drive up, doors slam, talking.

One man jumped out of his truck and sparked two bright red flares in the right-hand lane about fifty feet from the huge mangled buck, which someone was already pulling by a leg off the interstate. The deer's antlers left white trails as if a giant had scratched his nails against the asphalt like a chalkboard.

Will reached over instinctively. The seat was empty. He brushed deer hair off his face, and blood. He wasn't sure if it was the deer's blood or his own. "Oh my God. Oh my God. Oh my God!" he yelled.

He unfastened his seat belt, hurt, but still scooted over and patted the floorboard to see if the kid was there. Nothing.

"Oh my God. Oh my God. Oh my God," he said again.

He reached over the car seat to the back, almost jumped over, but felt a pain so severe in his stomach that he bent forward and threw up. He spat a few times and turned again, reached over the seat despite the pain. Touched Memo's legs, then Tony's. Yelled at them, "You guys all right?"

There was no answer. "René, René, you back there, hijito?"

There was no answer. He pulled himself over the seat as much as he could. The pain made him black out for a minute. He forced himself back to. Pulled himself over. Felt around the floor, around Memo's legs, over the hump in the middle, under Tony's legs. Nothing.

He pulled himself back into his seat, reached at the windshield, knew what he was looking for, knew there'd be a big hole. He could feel the unusually cool South Texas winter breeze before he made contact with the heated hood, then with what little glass was left along the edges, cut himself, blacked out again. Almost immediately he came back to, his hands on the hot hood. The headlight still bright. He imagined the huge hole in the red glow.

Someone was at the car door. "You all right? Everybody all right?"

"Yes . . . no, my kids . . . they're in the back. Check on 'em, please. The little one, René, I can't find him. Find him. Find him, please. I can't see. Please, help me find him." Will reached at the man's shirt and gripped it, then let go. "Help me, please, help me find the little one. Get the kids out of here, please. I smell gas. Do you smell gas? Please get them out of here. Get them some help. Do you have a phone? Call the cops . . . the ambulance. Please. Help the ones in the back, please."

The man at the door turned to listen to another person yelling something at him; Will's bloody hand was printed onto his shirt. You could see it clearly in the bright headlight lighting up the whole bloody scene.

The man walked off toward the person yelling at him. Will thought he heard the word "child." He pulled himself up, closer to the door to hear better, couldn't hold it, folded over. He slowly, painfully moved his hand back to the passenger's side, started feeling around in vain, again. His fingers brushed the handkerchief. He grabbed for it, knew immediately what it was, still folded, thick, took it in his other hand, put it to his face, breathed deeply. His other hand, back to searching aimlessly, found Jabba the Hut.

FLATBED

They could hear the fire engine coming for a long time before they could actually see it. The father cried. The mother, holding the youngest, an infant, a little boy, in her arms, cried too. Two others, another boy about nine, and a girl, six or seven and freckled, stood by the ranch fence, collecting pebbles to throw at each other.

"You're gonna get bit by a rattler," the father yelled at the two between sobs and wiping his face with a handkerchief. "And don't come a-running to me when you do."

They took after their mother, white as could be. No one ever believed him when he'd say proudly, "Yes, sir. They're my kids. All mine," especially when they'd go up into the panhandle to visit her family. Once, when they were visiting some relatives in Sweetwater, the boy, the oldest, around five or six years old, pulled down his shorts to show everyone a light brown birthmark that covered the back of his little thigh. He said, "See? Just like my daddy." Everyone who had come for miles from all over the county, some even from way past the cap rock, laughed at the kid. The faulty window unit made the air in the dark living room humid and heavy. Roberto laughed, too, nervously. Not a dark face around them, not even his kids.

But four years in South Texas had toughened their fair skin; it glowed a golden pink, like looking at the sun through the dried husk of early corn.

Roberto stared at what was left of the flatbed. Everything they owned packed tight and high had been covered with a $3.99 poly-urethane canvas from Walmart, then secured with a hundred feet of zigzagged yellow polyester rope he'd had for years but never used—all gone now, all charred, black, unrecognizable.

Roberto had flicked his cigarette butt out the window at the end of an old Hank Williams song he'd been singing for the kids.

Fire catches fast at sixty miles per hour.

When the kids and his wife had started yelling, he looked be-hind him through the rearview mirror at the blaze following them. The trailer hitched to the truck was overwhelmed by flames. He pulled over onto the shoulder of the road, made sure they got out of the truck safely, then made them stand far away, close to the barbed-wire fence. They watched.

"Look out for snakes!" he yelled, then left them there while he walked toward the road to meet the county fire truck. The fire had almost burned itself out. A fireman only had to douse the glow-ing embers to snuff it. Black smoke streaked against the baby-blue South Texas sky.

"What are we gonna do, Meagan?" Roberto said to his wife. They were back in the truck, headed into the underpass to the Shamrock station on the other side of the interstate.

"Well, motherfucking quit smoking for one," she answered. "I kept telling you not to throw the darn cigarette butts out the window. But I thought you'd start a *grass* fire. Not this, no, not this. How many times did I say it, huh? How many?" One of the flatbed trailer's four tires had popped from the heat of the fire. The rim screeched as they rolled onto the pavement of the Shamrock station.

"Jesus on the Cross," he answered.

"Stop swearing in front of the children, Robbie. I've told you over and over and over!" she yelled at him. "We ain't got nothing left. All gone. No beds for the kids. No refrigerator. No clothes, Robbie. Do you realize that? All we've got left of clothes is what we're wearing. The kids don't got nothing left, and they start school next week. What we gonna do now? You're an idiot. I can't believe you. Give me the fucking pack of cigarettes." She opened the door and stepped out of truck, the baby in her arms. The two other kids followed.

"Give 'em here," she snarled.

Roberto pulled the cigarettes reluctantly from his shirt pocket and handed them to her as he came around the front of the vehicle toward them. She threw the pack on the ground and smashed them with her sneaker.

He stared at the ground—not at what she was doing, just at the pavement in front of him.

"I start working tomorrow, Meagan," he said.

"You ain't gonna get paid for two weeks, Robbie, two weeks. What are we gonna to do till then, huh? How much you got in your wallet? Tell me."

"You know how much we have. You were with me when we cashed the last check at the groceries. Eight hundred went for the money order for the apartment—four hundred for the deposit and another four hundred for the first month's rent. That left us about two hundred. Thirty dollars for gas. We have about one hundred seventy-five dollars left, something like that. We'll go to Walmart.

Stuff's on sale now for back to school. We'll get the kids T-shirts and jeans for now. One pair of jeans each and two or three T-shirts. We'll get the baby some more diapers. Something for the kids to sleep in. They'll be all right, Meagan. They will. Look at 'em over there. They're playing, friggin' throwing rocks at each other. They're kids, Meagan. They'll be all right. I'll look for more jobs. Lots of building in San Antonio. Lots of work. The apartment's paid for for a month, Meagan. We got a roof over our heads." He looked down again, focused on the hot asphalt.

"Did you subtract the money you paid for the damn cigarettes, Robbie, huh? You subtract that?"

"Come on, Meagan, for heaven's sake. You ain't gotta be like that. You think I did it on purpose? You think I wanted to burn everything? You think I wanted to burn the kids' clothes, their toys? What the hell?" He started walking away from her, still staring at the ground, then said, "I gotta pee." He looked at the kids and yelled, "Stay away from the tall grass, kids. There's snakes out there. Don't think that just 'cause we're by the goddamn store that there ain't no snakes out there."

"Stop cursing, Robbie," Meagan yelled at him. "Stop cursing!"

"Goddammit," he said again, when he found the door of the bathroom locked. He made his way toward the store for the keys.

In the bathroom, door safely locked, he pulled a little plastic bag from the coin pocket of his jeans, laid it on the sink, then grabbed for his keys. He scooped some of the sticky yellow powder onto the key and held it to his nose, felt the sting in his nostrils, in his eyes, in his brain. He ran the water, dipped two fingers into the stream, then held his fingers up to his nose, snorted the water to push the shit down. He closed the lid on the toilet and sat down. Tried to gather his thoughts. "Fuck," he said, shook his head. *What the hell am I gonna do?* he thought. *And then I go and spend fifty bucks on this shit.*

He took another hit. Felt the sting again. Above him, the exhaust fan up by the light went on suddenly. It startled him. He sat on the toilet and put his hands to his face. He could still smell the burning; it floated in the air around him, followed him.

The speed up his nose intensified the smell of burn.

~

They met at the parking lot of the Alamo drag races one hot evening exactly nine summers ago, at the concession stand, under the T-shirt vendor's yellow light.

"I know that the T-shirts look a little off-color with the damn yellow light, but it's the only way I can keep these damn mosquitoes away. Y'know they have the malaria, I mean the damn West Nile virus," the vendor said to him when he'd finally stepped up and gotten the courage to ask her, "Which one you want? I'm buying."

She smiled at him and pointed at a red tank top that read *Smokin' Alamo Dragway* in fiery black letters. She couldn't stop looking at him, at the color of his skin; he was so sexy. She couldn't stop smiling. She felt a tingle between her legs when he finally reached in and play-punched her in the arm after a stupid joke about a blond. He swore to her he'd never seen a woman so white.

"I can see your veins, man," he said to her, touching her skin gently with his lazy finger. "I can see your blood pumping. That's amazing, man."

Not two weeks later, in that very parking lot, during the last race of the season, they fucked as if they were in a movie, hard and sweaty. She came as spinning tires burned rubber into smoke. He came right after she did, right as Jack Harris's Nitro-Thunder's chutes whooshed open.

They were quiet for a long time. He stayed inside her way past the yelling and the clapping, past the announcer's voice bidding them a good evening and a safe drive home. They finally stirred when they sensed the crowd walking around them; a kid cried because his dad wouldn't buy him a corn dog. "You wanna get all fat like your mom?" The kid's mother just turned around as she walked ahead of them and shot him the finger. Roberto could barely see them through the windows, tinted just one shade past legal.

She stayed pregnant on and off for the next eight years.

～

Someone knocked on the bathroom door. He panicked. Quickly shoved the baggie into the pocket of his jeans.

"Robert, what you doing in there?" asked Meagan. "Open the door."

"I'm coming. Hold on a second. I'm coming."

She heard the toilet flush, saw him walk out, stared at him.

"What were you doing in there, Robbie? What the hell were you doing in there?" The baby started crying.

"I was peeing, Meagan. What do you think I was doing in there?"

"I know what you were doing in there, Robbie. I can tell by your eyes. You're tweakin' again, aren't you, Robbie? Goddammit, Robbie. I can't believe you."

"I ain't doing it again, Meagan. I promise. I was crying, dammit. I just burned everything my family owned because of a stupid mistake, and you think I'm doing crank because my eyes are red? You're heartless, Meagan. Heartless." He sniffed. It stung.

"You better not be fucking doing it again, Robbie. I'll leave you.

I promise I don't care what happens to you. I'll take the kids and head back home. I promise, Robbie, you do that shit again, and I'm gonna leave you for good."

"Dammit, Meagan. Trust me, for Christ's sake. Trust me for once. I'm trying to do a good thing. I got myself another job. Got us an apartment. We're moving to the big city like you always wanted us to. Dammit, Meagan. Trust me, goddammit, trust me for once in your fucking life."

His eyes started watering now. The drip stung his throat. He sniffled, went with it, took his dirty handkerchief out of his back pocket again, wiped his tears, bowed his head.

"Okay, Robbie. Sorry. I'm sorry. I'm all worked up. I'm worried, y'know. What are we gonna do?"

"I told you, honey, we're gonna be all right. We got some money left, enough to buy some clothes for the kids, some food. The kids are starting school. They get the damn free breakfast and free lunches, don't they? We'll buy snacks and stuff for dinner. I'll get a couple of them blow-up mattresses for you and the kids in the meantime. I can sleep on the floor. I'll go downtown tomorrow morning, work all weekend doing day labor. Make a few extra dollars for us. We'll be all right—promise."

They heard the kids yelling, turned toward the field.

"What's going on over there?" he yelled. "You two get yourselves over here right away. You hear me?"

The kids came running toward them.

"I promise, Meagan. Believe me, we're gonna be all right. I can feel it. This is just a temporary thing, a temporary setback. I'm going back into the store right now and calling my dad's friend, you know, Mr. Perez, and I'm gonna ask him if he ain't got something I can do to make a few extra bucks on the side tomorrow, some cleanup somewheres, some paint job, fuck, cleaning bathrooms for alls I care, and if that don't work, I'll do day labor just like I said. We'll be all right. I promise."

"Daddy, can we buy a Coke? Can we buy a Coke? C'mon, Dad, we're thirsty. We'll share it. Promise. Me and Cindy'll share it, huh, Dad? Can we buy a Coke?"

Roberto stared at Meagan for direction.

"Sure, let 'em have a dollar. And don't be fighting for it once you get it. Share proper. Be good."

He reached into his pocket for some cash, and as he pulled his hand out, the crank slipped out and fell onto the pavement. He saw it fall. The kids held their hands out. Roberto looked at Meagan to see if she had seen it.

Baby at her waist, she stared at the crank on the ground, then up at Robbie, then away into the black smoke spun out across the blue sky, wondering how they ever got to this point. The blue sky made her think of her mamma, of the endless white of the cotton fields back home in West Texas, of the peace she'd known, it seemed, just a short time ago.

The kids didn't notice anything. They came back from the store fighting for the can of Pepsi and dropped it. Meagan and Roberto stood exactly where they were when the kids left to buy the soda. Meagan yelled, "Give it here!" The girl quickly picked it up, handed it to her mamma, and ran off.

Meagan couldn't even look at Roberto. She walked around him toward the back of the building where she sat on the sidewalk in the shade of the Dumpster. She put the near-empty can of soda to the baby's mouth and let a few drops trickle in. The baby licked the now-warm liquid. She said quietly, "My baby. Sweet, sweet baby." She stared at the baby's tongue, amazed at its fleshy pinkness. She remembered a bunch of baby mice she'd found back home once in her closet in a shoe box, squirming. *To be back home on my daddy's farm*, she thought.

The sun brightened, got hotter, it seemed. She swooned, felt faint. The baby grew heavy. She was sure she'd drop him. She mouthed the name "Robert," then mouthed "help me," but nothing came out.

She slowly raised the can of soda to her lips and let the last of the tepid liquid flow down her throat. She closed her eyes, took a deep breath, gathered her strength, and yelled out this time, "Robert!"

He came running round the corner, saw her struggle, helped her up.

"Give me a quarter, some change—anything."

He reached into his pockets, pulled out a handful of change, and poured it into her cupped hand.

"Meagan, look, I threw it away, flushed it down the toilet. All gone. Never, never again. Never. Promise," he said as he followed her to the store's entrance.

She stopped at the pay phone, leaned on the newspaper vending machine. She picked up the phone, put two quarters into the slot, and pressed 0. The operator answered. "I'd like to make a collect call, ma'am. Yes. Eight-oh-six, seven-nine-one, four-oh-nine-one. Meagan. Yes, ma'am, Meagan Ramirez. Thank you."

"Hello."

"Yes, this is the AT&T operator with a collect call from Meagan. Meagan Ramirez. Will you accept the charges?"

"Yes. Yes, ma'am. I accept."

"Go ahead."

"Meagan. Is that you? You all right?"

EL GATO

She hit him hard, elbowed him in the gut, whispered to him right up close, "Get the fuck away from me."

She could smell him, his familiar cologne, sweeter after a sweaty sleep. It revolted her now.

Still, even after she punched him, he followed closely behind her.

"Leave me the fuck alone, Joe."

He followed her into the walk-in closet. She ignored him now, scooped up half a row of clothes on hangers and dumped the load on the bed. Started folding. Packing.

"Don't be stupid, Carla. You're imagining it all. Nothing happened. Really. Look, Carla, it's not safe to drive to San Antonio all by yourself."

"What the fuck? What about the hairs, Joe? You think I'm an idiot? You took your pants off somewhere, Joe; that's the only way to get cat hair on your fucking underwear. You think I'm an idiot? I told you to get the fuck out of my face, Joe. Fuck you!" she yelled,

"Meow, meow, meow," and pulled the pair of underwear out of her pants pocket. "What about the fucking cum stains, huh? What about that?" She threw them at him. They hit his face.

⁓

She got in the car and slammed the door decidedly, resigned never to come back, but when she got to the corner, she panicked, rolled down the car window, and puked. She saw him in the rearview mirror still standing in the middle of the street, hands at his waist, pair of underwear hanging from one of them.

⁓

"What are chicken-fried French fries?"

"Well, ma'am, we take French fries, half-cook 'em in the fryer, take 'em out, roll 'em in flour, dip 'em in batter, then fry 'em up again. Dilley's claim to fame. Why, people come from all over the state to eat 'em. Even Bush—see right there," he said pointing to a newspaper clipping decoupaged onto a beveled piece of wood hanging on the wall, "even President Bush had an order when he came down here to hunt whitetail with the Carters last Christmas. See? We serve 'em with cream gravy."

"Give me an order. I'm gonna walk across the parking lot to the little store over there. I'll be right back. I just have to buy something."

"Sure thing, ma'am. I'll put the order in right now, and they'll prolly be ready by the time you get back. Doesn't take too long to cook 'em," the young man said.

Carla walked out of the café and across the hot asphalt into the air-conditioned coolness of Martinez Mini-Mart. She stopped for a moment just inside the doors, and took a deep breath. She was perspiring now. Decidedly, she made her way up to the two young girls chatting at the checkout counter and asked quietly, "Do you sell pregnancy tests?"

When she got back, small plastic bag in hand, Carla made her way into the cedar-walled dining room. She spotted a booth after her eyes adjusted to the darkness—bright, South Texas sun still vibrating in her vision—and she sat down. She rolled the ticket stub the kid had handed her when she walked back into the restaurant, repeated her order number over and over to herself so as not to forget it, so as to focus, so as to forget him.

"Fifty-nine, ma'am. Order number fifty-nine." The kid stood in front of her, handed her the chicken-fried French fries in a green plastic basket lined with two sheets of restaurant paper spotted with oil. "Thought I'd bring 'em out to you. Can I get you a sodie?"

"No, thank you . . . thank you very much for . . . for bringing me my food."

"Okay, ma'am. Let me know if you need somethin' else."

"Okay . . . okay. Um . . . can I please get some water?" she asked as he turned away.

"Sure, I'll get you a nice, tall glass of water in a zip."

She didn't eat very much. Dipped a few of the fat fries into the little paper cup of gravy. Gulped her water. Asked for a refill. Drank that too.

She got up to get a newspaper someone had left on the table across from the row of booths. It was a Spanish-language paper she noticed. She slid back into the booth, unfolded the paper, stared dumbstruck. The lead story, bannered across the top, read MAN ARRESTED FOR SELLING TAMALES MADE WITH CAT MEAT.

She felt faint, sick, horrified. She pulled a twenty from her pocketbook and left it on the table, paperweighted it with the basket of fries. Walked to the door. Mouthed a thank-you to the kid behind the counter, then, "Left the money on the table. Thanks."

"Thank you, ma'am. You enjoy the fries?" he asked as she walked through the door, too quickly to hear him.

She was perspiring heavily, she noticed, as she walked to the car. The heat. The bright sun. The car seat was so hot, she had to wait a bit before entering. She started the engine and immediately cranked on the air-conditioner, smelled his cologne coming through the vents. She started hyperventilating, then gathered her thoughts, stepped on the gas. She sped out; dust rose behind her, pebbles flew. She drove for a mile on the access road before she could get back on the interstate. And when she finally did, she pulled over right past the on-ramp to throw up again. Bitter bile made its way up into her nose, stung. Chunks of chicken-fried French fries coughed out of her mouth, creamy saliva dangled from her lips to the heated asphalt.

Cat tamales. It's all she could think of. She thought she'd never eat again. Then the cat hair, the fucking cat hair on his underwear. She cried because she was so angry, lost, alone. Door open, head close to the ground so as not to splash inside her car, she felt dazed. The sun was no help either.

She talked to herself, "You really need to get your shit together." Pulled herself back up into the car. Fumbled through the glove compartment for some wipes. Wiped herself clean. Got back on the road.

She stared directly ahead of her, started counting the white stripes. Messed up on thirty-nine. Stopped counting. Felt lost for a moment. Stared at the mirage way up there. Almost started counting again. Then for a bit she thought she was on the highway to Monterrey, Mexico. She was flustered. Mad. Had to shake her head violently to change the scenery in front of her to what it really was, the highway between Laredo and San Antonio, not Mexico. Cat tamales.

Someone in a car in the other lane honked at her, woke her from her reverie. She'd been veering.

Oh my God oh my God oh my God, she thought.

She pulled over, parked the car far past the shoulder on the field of dry Texas wild grass, rested her head on the steering wheel.

She decided she couldn't drive anymore. Got back on the road, and at the first exit, got off and turned back around toward Dilley. She'd get a room there. There were a couple of motels right next to the road by the restaurant and the little store. *They looked decent*, she thought, then realized she didn't care what the hell they were like. She needed to take a pill, go to sleep, stop thinking, start again tomorrow.

Her cell phone rang. It was his ring. She reached over. Turned it off.

~

"Well, you're not gonna believe this, ma'am, but some pretty famous people have stayed here," said the woman at the front desk. "Yes, the Righteous Brothers, they stayed here when they played for the class reunion of the class of '69 . . . that's right, Dilley High. Shoot 'em up, Cowboys." She brandished finger pistols in the air in front of her. "As a matter of fact, I'm gonna give you the very room they stayed in. You like that, miss? Huh . . . you like that? Sign for me right here, please, hon, yeah, right there."

"Yes . . . um . . . yes . . . that's nice. Listen, I'm sorry. I'm really tired. I need to sleep. Just want to make sure the room is quiet."

"Absolutely. The room is super quiet. Are you all right, hon? Can I get you a soda or an Alka-Seltzer or somethin'? You look a little pale, hon, a little spooked. You all right?" she asked.

"No, thanks. Yes . . . yes, I'm okay. Just really tired. But thank you. Thanks a lot."

She walked back into the heat, got back in her car, and drove up to the parking space in front of the room. There were about ten other cars in the lot. She could see the communal pool on the other side of the hotel. A couple of families played in the water. Made her feel safe. She could barely hear the kids' yells. In her head, she thanked the woman at the front desk for her consideration. She pulled the bag with her toiletries from the backseat; her sleeping pills were in it. Walked into the motel room.

The room was cold. She shivered, then fumbled with the knobs on the air-conditioning unit right next to the door, floor level, under the window, and turned it from high to low. Rubbed her arms warm. She grabbed her medicine bag from her overnighter, pulled out her sleeping pills, put two under her tongue. At the sink at the other end of the room by the bathroom, she unwrapped a plastic cup and filled it with water to swallow the pills—which had already started dissolving—and undressed.

She turned on the TV, watched *Wheel of Fortune*, tried to solve the puzzle. "Remember, it's a thing," said Pat. "You want to spin or solve?"

She couldn't believe it was already past four-thirty in the afternoon. And it must have been from fatigue—for surely the pills couldn't work so fast—but she started blinking, that same blinking when you can't keep your eyes open any longer, and she fell asleep.

～

She woke up in the middle of the night, red LED light at 3:37 a.m., the TV gone to infomercials, blaring. She sat up in a panic, felt as if the top of her head was on fire. She got out of bed and, with only the light of the TV, found her way to the sink, stared at herself in the mirror for a minute while she filled the sink with cold water. She plunged her face under, and after a minute, straightened up, let the water drip down her body, puddle at her feet, cool her. Outside, she could hear two cats fighting . . . or fucking . . . she wasn't sure which.

CRANK

He was fucking scared. No shit. Really scared. Although he was in his midthirties, he'd never done such a thing before—picked up a woman at a bar, driven her crosstown to the West Side to buy drugs. Never. Never even done coke himself. But he did what she wanted him to. He was horny. Hadn't had a girlfriend for over a year now, and had been with the last for twelve years. He wasn't lucky with the ladies either—always told his friends, "No, you don't understand, I have to chat them up first. I have to charm them."

But that night, he didn't have much of a choice; testosterone had taken over, and although there were slim pickings, he made his move to the end of the bar where she stood. She had a thumb hooked into the pocket of her jeans, and in her other hand, she held a cigarette over the ashtray on the bar. It was late—closing time. The barkeep announced last call. And rather quickly—it had been easier than he had thought it would be—they left the bar together, and he found himself driving farther and farther away from familiar territory. She asked him to get money for the dope. He drove to the closest bank and withdrew forty bucks, guaranteeing, he thought, he'd get laid.

"Lights off!" she said softly, as if that would get him to turn the lights off quicker. "Turn your lights off and pull over. Yeah, right there, man. I see him. Ahí esta. Good. We lucked out."

He coasted to a stop. "Where?"

"Over there. *Shhh* . . . I'll be right back."

She opened the door, closed it really carefully, a quick click maybe, without a sound, and walked over to a car parked on the other side of the street, a little behind where they had rolled to a stop. Through the rearview mirror, he saw the car's door open slowly. A man stepped out, a gun stuck into his pants right above a big, silver belt buckle, like a rodeo champion. The handgun sparkled in what little light shone from the moon shrouded in silvery clouds.

The windows fogged up quickly, the air hot with alcohol and adrenaline. Inside the cab of the truck, it smelled like bedrooms smell in the mornings after two really drunk people have sex.

He was scared. "And all for pussy, all for pussy," he whispered, eyes darting from the rearview mirror to the mirror on the driver-side door, then ahead of him.

⌒

Suddenly she tapped at the window as he zoned, drunk, focusing on what he thought was someone inside a car two cars ahead. He twitched, then adjusted his vision, squinted to make out her face through the clouded window, had to double-check; the street lamp had been shot out. Her earring clinked against the glass.

He rolled down the window. Even in this dark craziness, she looked beautiful, like a movie star, like a young Sophia Loren.

Thumb hooked into her jeans pocket again. She had sad eyes, he thought, pleading and lost.

"Give me the money, man."

"What? How much, how much?"

"Twenty, thirty, whatever. C'mon, man. He's waiting."

"Well, I'm a little uncomfortable—"

"*Shhh* . . . just give me the money, man, come on." She placed her hand on his mouth, pressed down hard like she meant business. It hurt a little. "*Shhh* . . . just gimme the money, man. He's waiting. I gotta give him some money now or he's gonna get mad at the *both* of us. C'mon."

Her teeth clenched tight.

The urgency in her voice scared him. He fumbled through his shirt pocket, into which he had shoved the bills, and pulled out the two twenties, crisp, folded in half, fresh out of the ATM.

I'm gonna die. Dear Jesus, I'm gonna die, he thought, his upper jaw still smarting from her forceful grip.

She quickly counted the money he gave her and went back to the car across the street.

"Thank you, God. Gracias, Jesucristo Redentor." She was jonesing, jonesing really bad.

"Here, babe, two big rocks. Smoke 'em, man. Break 'em up a little, then smoke 'em. You'll get the most mileage that way. It's good stuff. Promise. Good stuff."

"Thanks, Johnny Boy. You're my man. You always got my back. Thanks, man."

"Hey, Sonia—do me a favor. Don't bring that dude back here no more."

"No, Johnny Boy. He's cool. Promise. He's cool. He's all square, man. He works at a bank. Don't worry."

"Don't bring 'im here no more. Okay, mi morenita?"

"Okay, papacito. Love you, man."

She put two fingers to her lips to flick him a kiss and went back to the truck. He would've hurt her if she would've come here with no money—not badly, but he would have slapped her a couple of times. She knew it. She'd seen him do it.

But she was beautiful, and this had always helped her.

He acts all nice and all, but he'd hurt me, just like that, she thought as she walked back to the passenger's side.

In one hand she held the dope in a tight, tight fist; the thumb of her other hand was hooked into her jeans pocket.

"Thank you, Jesus." She made the sign of the cross, and at the end, right at the end of the sign of the cross, right when she usually kissed her thumb as if holding the cross hanging at the end of a rosary, just as her mother had taught her to do, she kissed the sweet little plastic pouch and jumped back into the truck.

Once in, she put her face to her shoulder, smelled her underarm. "Damn, I still smell like fish," she said. "I gotta quit that job, I swear. Let's get the hell outta here."

She leaned over, kissed him, slipped him some tongue, let him know she was grateful for the money, for the ride, for bringing her all the way across town, and sat back. The dope was in her hands. She could feel it there. It reassured her. Made her happy.

He put the truck in gear and drove off slowly, didn't turn the lights on until the end of the block. He'd gotten the picture. He wasn't stupid.

She checked her underarm again. "Do I smell like fish? You know, fried fish. You know, like my work. Do I smell like Long John Silver's?"

He wrung the steering wheel. "No, you don't smell like fish."

"I told you I work at Long John Silver's, right?"

He nodded yes, kept his eyes on the road, afraid to get stopped. He thought, *I'm not only drunk, but there's drugs in the car now too. Fuck.*

He had just wanted to loosen her up. Never thought it would be this dangerous. He could've gotten held up, hurt, the truck stolen. *But no. Had to go along with it, didn't I?* he thought. *I gotta get home. Gotta get home. Gotta get home. Gotta get home.*

"I have a degree, you know. Sí, a associate's degree in food management. That's right, from St. Philip's College on the East Side. You know, right? You know St. Philip's, right?"

"Yes."

"I graduated in May. My grades weren't so hot. But I finished, didn't I?"

"Yes."

"What bank you work at?"

He thought up a lie, afraid now of the guy back there in the car, of her ilk.

"I work in real estate at the bank. Don't really have anything to do with money."

"Ooh, good. Yeah, me, I'm a homeowner. That's what you mean by real estate, right?"

She pulled a cigarette out of her bag and lit up.

She didn't even ask me, he thought. He wanted to tell her not to smoke in his truck. Decided not to.

Be careful. Slow down, he thought. They got to a busy intersection. *Slow down, slow down*, he kept thinking.

"Take Thirty-Five. Take the expressway," she said. "I really gotta pee."

"I can't get on the expressway right now, like this. I'm drunk. Too many cops. Can you hold it for ten minutes? We'll be at my house in ten minutes."

"Can't you pull over and let me pee? Just over there. Look, it's dark. Pull over, man. I gotta pee."

"I promise. We're five minutes from my house now. Okay? You okay with that?"

"Okay. Okay."

She really didn't have to pee, just wanted to get to his house and smoke the crank. He knew it and started getting angry, feeling upset, used. But just then, just as he turned the corner, her purse rolled over and popped open. He saw it in there, clear as day, a knife, a big one, a switchblade. So he shut up.

She looked at him as she grabbed her purse, put it back in order. Leering at him. Hating him for not pulling over. *For such a smart man, banker, real-estater, whatever, he's a fucking idiot*, she thought. *Look at him, such a sissy, all scared and all. I ain't gonna hurt you, honey. I just wanna smoke a little of this shit, man. I just wanna get out and smoke a little of this shit. Fuck him. Like he can't pull over for just a minute? How much longer? How much longer?*

"Hey, how much longer?"

"See that white house over there . . . on the right? That's my house." They pulled into the driveway. "Relax, we're here, we're here."

Yeah, shit, you relax with these little candies in your hand, mother-fucker, she thought, *you fucking relax*. She was turning into a fiend, a monster, someone he had not recognized in that dark bar.

She jumped out of the truck and waited for him at the door. "Come on, man, I gotta pee, please hurry."

"I'm coming. I'm coming. Don't make such a commotion. It's late. The neighbors—"

"You wanna fucking commotion? You wanna see what a com-motion really is?" she asked rather loudly.

He got the picture, hurried and unlocked the door, switched on the light.

She slipped in. "Where's your toilet?"

"Straight ahead, just straight ahead. You'll see the door."

Just take the damn stuff, and then I'm gonna get you out of here quickly, he thought. *I promise, Jesus, get me out of this one, and I'll never do it again, never. Promise.*

She came out of the bathroom rather quickly. He didn't even hear the toilet flush.

"Do you have foil? Tin foil? I need some foil."

"What for?"

"To smoke this stuff. Come on. Get the foil."

"You smoke it? I thought you were supposed to snort that stuff?"

"Can you get the foil, please? You don't even know what this is, do you?"

He went to the kitchen to get foil. He wanted to find it, was desperate to find it, take it back to her, let her smoke her damn stuff, then get her the hell out of the house. He grabbed the box and rushed back to the dining room where she sat at the table.

"Hey, get me a little plate, okay, just a little one, like a coffee plate, you know, like for under a cup of coffee."

He ran back to the kitchen, pulled a saucer out of the dishwasher, and ran back to the dining room.

She opened her hand. The little plastic baggie was stuck to her palm. She peeled it off, struggled with the tiny ziplock, finally opened it, and carefully poured the two large crystals onto the plate.

"Give me the foil."

He handed her the box.

She reached for her purse, which she had set on the chair next to her. Pulled out the switchblade.

He jumped back.

She giggled, "Hey, man, don't worry, man. I'm just gonna break this shit up, man. What'd you think? I was gonna slice you up, man? C'mon, man. You're silly, silly, real silly." She stared at him, pressed the button and the blade switched open. She broke one of the crystals in two—*clink.*

"Fuck the foil," she said, and went back into her purse for her pack of cigarettes. She pushed the half a crystal that looked like rock salt into the tip of the cigarette. Lit up. Her eyes rolled back into her head. They were solid white for a while, almost pearlescent, almost beautiful.

"Take a hit," she said. "Let me load it for you. Here. Look . . ."

"No, not really. Don't do that. Thanks. You do it all."

She pressed hard on the second half a crystal to break it up into smaller pieces, the blade flat on it this time, and when she did so, a few grains spilled off the plate onto the floor.

"Oh my God. What did I do? How much fell?" She pushed off the table and fell immediately to her hands and knees, touching the ground as if blind. Then she looked up at him suddenly, crazed, and asked, "Is somebody back there? Are the cops back there?"

Dammit, she's wigging out, he thought. "No, there's nobody back there. Promise."

"Let's go see."

"Okay." He took her to the back of the house, past the bathroom. Walked her through both bedrooms. Showed her the closets. Pulled up the dust ruffle from around each bed. Made her look underneath. "See? No one's in here. I promise. No one's in here."

"What about outside? They're waiting outside, aren't they, the police?"

"No!" he said loudly, almost yelling, exasperated. "Come and see for yourself." He pulled the curtain aside, pulled up the blind. Nothing there, she saw. Just a backyard. Plain backyard. Not even a dog.

Then, she looked at him, dazed, stoned, and slurred, "I thought your house was bigger, you know, being a banker and all." She turned away from him and started walking, slowly, headed back to the dining room, almost as if she were floating, sat down at the table, but in the chair opposite of the one she'd been sitting in.

"So I can look back there," she said, pointing to the back of the house. "Wanna make sure no one's back there. You sure no one's back there?"

He stared at her. Started hating her.

She smoked the rest of the crank. With every hit, her eyes rolled back into her head. Smoked it all except for two crystals still on the saucer.

He started wondering if she hadn't been casing the house, acting wasted, paranoid, looking for vulnerable places, entries, windows her gun-toting friend could come and break in through in the middle of the night, kill him. *For what?* he thought, *my TV, my computer, my DVD player, my poor dead mother's silver?* He thought Johnny Boy might even be on his way over already, right now. He trembled, barely, but visibly now, visibly, at least to him— angry, truly afraid for his life. She puffed away.

"Positive," he said. "You saw yourself. No one's back there."

He was now beginning to think that she was going to overdose. She'd smoked so much. It seemed too much. He'd never done it, but he knew what speed could do to a person. He'd seen the movies. Seen the special report on *Nightline*, "Methamphetamine: The New Killer Drug." He imagined her heart pumping, faster and faster, harder and harder, then stopping. Just like that. He closed his eyes. *Should I call an ambulance? What'll I do if she OD's? How do I explain it to the police? Jesus, help me*, he thought.

"Haven't you smoked enough of that stuff?" he asked.

She looked at him, one eye closed, "What? You pay for this shit?" Then she giggled, remembered that he had. "Just kidding, amigo, just kidding. Sit down with me." Stoned. Wasted. Gone. "Here. Come. . . . Sit right here, my sweet papaya. Close to me." She patted her hand on the seat of the chair next to hers.

She pulled another cigarette from her purse, pushed the last two pieces of rock into the tip.

He sat down.

She caressed the inside of his thigh, made her way up to his crotch. Smiled sweetly. Lit up.

～

"Why are you so quiet?" she asked him, coming out of her stupor, as she had done a few times during the ride to get her home, a few times enough to let him know where to take her. Back to the same neighborhood they'd been the night before. He thought about dropping her off at a bus stop, dumping her. It would've been easy enough; she seemed so lifeless, wasted. But he couldn't do it. He'd take her home even if it meant going back to that part of town. He'd take her home. Get rid of her. Anything to get rid of her.

"I'm tired—that's all," he answered. No interest in talking with her—he was angry, really angry now that the sun was out, now that it was light, now that he felt safe.

"Hey, don't worry. I know lots of guys who can't get it up sometimes. No big deal. Get some Viagra," she said to him rather lucidly, giggled. This made him even angrier.

He pulled down the visor; the strong, early-morning South Texas sun blinded him. He could barely see where he was going. Even now, he was still a little drunk. In shock. Even now, he was nervous. Edgy. Knew he wouldn't be all right until she was out of the truck. Away from him. His life. His home. Away from him.

She nodded off again.

"Hey! Wake up," he said to her a few blocks later, shook her rather severely, a little too hard. "You have to tell me where we're going. Wake up! Don't fall asleep."

She opened her eyes slightly, dazed. "Where are we? Oh, yeah, up there. I see. Up there. Take a left on Zarzamora. Just up there. Yeah, right up there. Up there," she repeated, pointing in no particular direction. "Yeah, one more block. Right here. Turn. Right there. Yeah, just right there on the left. Yeah, drop me off right there. That's my mamma's house. She's dead now. Dead. She left it to me. The house, that house, the white one with the red roof. Qué pretty, right? Yeah, that one. Right here."

She leaned over, tried to kiss him. He turned away. She laughed, got out slowly, slammed the door shut.

KILLER DOG

The next day, his dog was dead.

He was driving home from the supermarket, where he'd gone to buy dog food because he'd run out that morning. He lived on the outskirts of the ritzy neighborhood Los Alamos, even shared the same last two digits of the zip code with the rich folk—and the ritzy supermarket—but that's as far as it went. He lived in the poor section, the one close to services—you know, dry cleaners, all-night diners, the apartments for university students, car wash/ garage/oil change places, the back entrance to the country club. But when he'd fed the dog in the morning, he heard the last few chunks clink into the metal bowl. He remembered he needed dog food on his way back home from work, just a few blocks from his house, as he drove in front of the snob-market.

When he turned the corner a few feet from his house, there was his dog, Nelson, in the middle of the street, jumping up at two women. Both screamed frantically, and one of them fell to the ground and flicked a Bic lighter at the dog's face, over and over, as if to defend herself.

"That damn dog attacked us. Your damn dog attacked us!" she yelled at him. She'd seen him get out of his car to get the dog in the house.

"Call the cops!" yelled one of them, T-shirt pulled up, big belly exposed, pants so tight they had chafed around her waist like a belt.

"Just call them on your cell, Gracie, nine-one-one!" she yelled to the other, then to him, "That damn dog of yours attacked us."

"But he's a puppy. He was just playing with you. He looks big, but he's a puppy, really."

"Puppy, my ass."

"I'm telling you, he's a puppy. I have his papers if you want to see how old he is. Did he bite you? No, of course not. You think that huge dog wouldn't have bitten you if he wanted to?"

"Just call the cops, Gracie. Sue him."

"Sue me? The dog didn't even do anything to you."

"What do you mean? He threw me down."

"But you're not hurt. Look at you. You're fine."

"Look, mister, we're calling the cops. Just keep your damn killer dog away from us."

"Killer dog? Away from you? He's already inside the house. He's in the backyard."

The cops came—two of them. One of them played with the dog in the backyard.

"Ma'am, that dog's just a puppy, and he seems like a really nice dog."

"I don't care. He attacked us."

"Officer, he didn't attack them . . . he jumped on them like he jumped on you when you went back there. He's just a puppy. I saw it all. I was driving back from the groceries. I saw it happen right there in the middle of the street. Yes, he did jump on her, but not in a bad way. He was just playing. When I saw what was going on, I parked the car on the curb, look, right there, and I called the dog. He came right to me, but she was already on the pavement. I went to help her after I put the dog in the house. He's a year and half. He's a puppy and a sweet dog, but he started jumping the chain link fence two or three days ago, and I didn't want to have to tie him up."

"Well, you should. He could've killed me."

"Ma'am, I'm sorry, and I'll file a report if you'd like me to, but I've played with the dog, and I can't imagine him trying to hurt you."

"Go ahead, write him the report. You're not gonna give him a ticket?"

"Ma'am, he's got a collar and he's got a tag. It wasn't like he was walking him without a leash or anything. The dog jumped over the fence."

"Well, can you give him a ticket?"

"No, ma'am, I can't. But I'll write up the complaint."

"Good. Write him up. Write him up good, real good."

The cop looked at him and rolled his eyes.

~

The next day, his dog was dead.

All around the yard, in the grass, the dog had scratched these trenches, as if it had been digging frantically from pain.

The two women had come back again in the middle of the night and stealthily thrown a poisoned T-bone into the backyard.

He found the chewed, fleshy bone by the chain link fence between the yard and the driveway.

~

He called the city to find out what to do with the dog's body, and the woman who took his call seemed nice, even consoling. She told him that he should put the dog's body in front of the house in a box, and that workers would pick the dog up that very afternoon. It was strange to place the dog for pickup on the sidewalk as if he were trash, as if it were Trash Day. That's when he finally cried over the phone to the woman from city services.

The dog was heavy, dead. It was hard to get him into the air-conditioner box he'd stored in the garage earlier that summer when he switched out the busted window unit in the living room. He took the old air-conditioner out of the box and pushed it into a corner where it'd be out of the way until Bulky Item Collection Day the following month. Then he'd take it out onto the curb, just like his dog, for pickup.

He had a hard time getting the dog's body in. He had to turn the box on its side and push/slide the dog in. When he finally did, he flipped the box upright and dragged it to the front of the house. The dog was stiff already and his legs stuck out the top. He had to push them down then close the flaps and weigh them down with a broken brick he'd used to prop open one of the garage doors.

He guessed the dog had been dead most of the night, and it was already half-past noon.

~

Two weeks later there was a huge thunderstorm, and the house's old wiring blew a fuse. He had gone home for Labor Day weekend to see his family in the valley, and when he returned late that Monday night, the whole house smelled of rotting flesh.

In the fridge, a brisket his mom had given him had spoiled in its plastic vacuum packaging. The plastic wrapper had expanded like a balloon and popped. He wet a towel and held it over his nose and mouth, the smell was so bad. He pulled the meat out, dumped it into a trash bag, and shook a box of baking soda into the freezer before shutting the door.

His mom had packed the giant piece of meat in ice for him so carefully. Froze it solid for several days. Even bought a $3.99 Styrofoam cooler from the Walmart so he could bring it back with him. He did. He couldn't imagine eating so much meat. He remembered thinking he'd feed it to the dog.

He figured he'd put the meat out on the curb with the trash like he did every Sunday night, right where he had placed Nelson's box not two weeks before. But when he walked back to the front door from the curb, he could still smell the rotting meat. He was sure his neighbors could smell it too. Windows now open to a rare South Texas breeze, he was sure the smell was wafting into their homes.

So instead, he carried the slab of meat to the back of the house on a shovel, then he dug a hole in the far back corner of the backyard to bury the brisket. He imagined the neighbors peeking out their windows, sniffing, smelling the rotting meat and imagining he'd killed somebody, dismembered the victim, and was now disposing of the body in pieces.

He dug deep.

⌒

Three days later, off work at noon, he went to the backyard and pulled the hose from under the wooden steps that led up to the kitchen door to rinse away the huge puddle of blood the dog had left on the floor of his wooden shed where he'd found his body bleeding at both ends. He sprinkled Ajax unceremoniously over the pool of blood that had already set, dark and hard around the edges. He hosed it down. He scrubbed at the edges with what was left of an old broom the dog used to chew on.

CUT YA

She got off the couch again and made her way to the door to let in some skinny kid and told him to wait while she made sure the door was locked behind him. She sent the kid upstairs and made her way back into the living room where Julian sat in an over-stuffed green velvet chair opposite where she and another drag queen had been sitting on a matching sofa. He'd only been there for maybe twenty minutes, and already three people had come to the door looking for drugs.

She shuffled right up to him and asked, "Are you a cop? Huh? Are you a cop? 'Cause if you are, I'll cut ya."

He said, "No."

She said again, "'Cause if you are, I'll cut ya," and cut the air with an imaginary knife in hand.

He didn't know whether to laugh or cry.

"No," he repeated. "My name's Julian. Nice to meet you. Teresa brought me here, remember? She said it was okay."

"Yeah, yeah, whatever. I'm Rita. And if you're a cop, I'll cut ya," she said again, and she and the other drag queen sitting on the giant couch laughed.

All he wanted was some crank, but he hadn't been able to find any at the gay bar where he'd gotten it a couple of times before, at the recommendation of a college friend. So this drag queen, Teresa, a big Mexican American *girl* from Lubbock, Texas, said, "I'll make a phone call." And she did. "Do you mind driving a bit? We have to go up north on Thirty-Five to get it."

After the bar closed and they had all walked out like cattle at a Texas roundup, he helped her into his truck, her beehive hairdo so high she had to push it down to fit.

On their way to get the drugs, a police car drove up next to them. She waved dramatically at the cop. The policeman laughed and sped away. Julian squeezed the steering wheel nervously.

When they got to the apartment complex, Rita answered the door cautiously, then let them in. Teresa quickly disappeared up the stairs and left him with Rita and the other drag queen sitting on the big green velvet couch in the living room.

Rita told him, "Sit there," and pointed at the chair he flopped onto. He sat for a few minutes without saying anything while Rita fiddled with the remote control, channel-surfing the TV.

Someone knocked again. She threw the remote at him and got up to answer the door, "Choose something."

After she'd answered the door and sent this visitor up the stairs too, she went back to the couch and pulled at a backpack at her feet and brought out a glass pipe. Then she reached back into the bag and pulled out a little plastic bag filled with white crystals.

Holy mother of God, he thought. *Is she going to spark it up right here? What if someone knocks on the door again?* She apparently didn't care.

The other drag queen, the one sitting next to her on the couch, said, "I wish I would've died today. I think I almost did. I wish I would just die."

"Well, die already," said Rita, and they both laughed.

Julian fidgeted with the sixty dollars rolled in his pocket that he'd gotten for the stuff.

He looked at her, squinting because the light from the low-watt lamp hanging from the ceiling in the far corner of the room wasn't enough to see her easily. He hadn't noticed because of her heavy makeup at first, but after she spoke, she sounded tired and weak. That's when he realized she was sick—sick-sick. The sick one bit off her fake nails and spat them into an ashtray between the two of them.

"Oh, thank you," Rita said, and reached into the ashtray for one of the clippings. She shoveled some speed from the plastic bag into the pipe with it.

She yelled, "Who the fuck has a lighter?"

"I don't smoke," he said.

Someone upstairs threw a lighter down. It landed at his feet. He picked the lighter off the dirty green shag carpet and handed it to her.

She put the pipe to her mouth and sucked hard. He was amazed at how much smoke the little bit of speed could make. She exhaled a huge cloud of wispy smoke into the air. It smelled like chemicals—a strange, acrid scent, sour-sweet. She reached for the nail clipping she had put back into the ashtray and scooped some more powder into the pipe. She handed it to him with the lighter.

"No," he said. "I've never smoked it."

"Well, how do you do it?" she asked. "You shoot up?"

"No," he said. "I usually put it up my nose or eat it."

She said, "Okay," and put the pipe and lighter down, grabbed the nail clipping and the baggie, and walked over to him. She scooped some stuff out of the bag and said, "Here," and put the clipping to his nose so he could snort it. He did. It burned like hell.

She said, "Smoke some. It's better. You'll like it."

He said, "No, thanks. I gotta drive and I don't know what it'll do to me. Where's Teresa?"

She yelled up the stairs, "Teresa, your little boyfriend down here's getting tired of waiting for your fat ass. I'm going to have to take him from you if you don't come down here soon. . . . Teresa? . . . Bitch? You hear me?"

He smiled when she winked at him.

She reached again into the tiny plastic bag for more shit and walked back to him and again put the nail clipping to his nose. He snorted, closed his eyes, and leaned his head on the back of the chair.

He opened his eyes after the stinging stopped. Teresa walked down the stairs, wasted. "Ay, honey," she said, "I'm so sorry I took so long, but they kept giving me drugs up there. No, really, I'm so sorry. But look," she continued, reaching into her bra to pull out a little plastic bag, fat with crystals. "For you. Hey, I know I took a long time up there, baby, and if you don't feel like taking me all the way home, if you gotta get home or whatever, I can stay here, really, no big deal, no big deal at all."

"No way," he said, "I'll take you home." He pushed the baggie into the coin pocket of his jeans after she handed it to him.

Rita, dazed, got off the couch to walk them out and secure the door. He now figured it was her job. At the door, Rita kissed him on the cheek, and Teresa said, "Bitch, get away from my man."

He had to help Teresa walk to the truck because she was so wasted and because she was wearing four-inch heels. She stopped suddenly in the middle of the street. He glanced at his watch. It was 4:34 in the morning.

Teresa shoved her wrist to his face. She pointed at a bracelet about four inches wide of solid rhinestones that she had been wearing all night. "You like this?" she asked.

"Yes," he said.

She slipped it off and pointed at the inside of the bracelet to show him it was made of cardboard, just a plain piece of cardboard tubing, like from a mailing tube, but covered with rhinestones.

"Hot glue. Seventy fucking dollars worth of rhinestones. You think it's worth it?" she asked, her eyes rolling slightly back into her head. He grabbed her gently by the arm when she took a step back, afraid she'd fall, walked her back to the truck, and helped her back in.

"It looked really good on stage, Teresa," he said. "It looked really, really beautiful."

VACATION

He stared intently at the road sign just ahead to the right. His wife squatted outside the car to pee. Although the door was ajar to screen her from oncoming traffic, it did nothing to shield her from the cars and the trucks and the eighteen-wheelers that were traveling north on I-35. The sign was government green, and its white, pearlescent letters sparkled like Christmas lights every time the beacon atop the prison tower on the other side of the road swung around. In the twilight, the prison looked like a giant, windowless La Quinta Motor Inn surrounded by razor-wired electric fencing that stretched for a mile.

PRISON AREA
DO NOT PICK UP HITCHHIKERS

He could hear her peeing. It sounded like water flowing from the filter of the aquarium in their bedroom back home.

He watched her pee, stared right at her, knew this would enrage her. The stream of urine reflected the bright red flash of the emergency blinkers he had switched on so no one would crash into them.

"Don't look at me," she said, annoyed.

He imagined an eighteen-wheeler smashing into them at seventy miles per hour. "What a way to go," he said softly and giggled at the thought.

"What did you say?" she asked. Her eyes flashed red when the tower light swung around again.

"Nothing," he answered.

"Can you get me the wipes, please?" she said angrily. "They're in the glove compartment."

"Get 'em yourself," he answered.

"Dammit, Victor, just get me the fucking wipes, for Christ's sake," she pleaded, unable to move much.

A man in a pickup—zigzagging a bit, drunk—slowed down, honked, then whistled a loud catcall after catching her silhouette in the headlights of his old, beat-up truck.

She wanted to shoot him the finger but didn't, couldn't really.

Victor laughed out loud.

He then reached over from the driver's side and popped open the glove compartment. He searched under car manual and map and flashlight and tire gage and endless sticky wrappers of bite-size Snickers that she'd been eating throughout the trip until he found the baby-blue plastic container. The box was warm; the scent in the air, sweet.

He threw it at her so hard it put her off-balance, pushed her from the delicate, uncertain position she had been holding butt-first into the puddle of hot urine.

She sat in the puddle for four swings of the revolving light. Counted—one, two, three, four—until she grabbed the door

handle and pulled herself back up into position. She was now crying she was so furious.

She reached right under the car where the wipes had fallen,
grabbed the container, and pulled several napkins out. She, too,
noticed they were warm, then wiped, reaching twice with her free
hand, once to remove a sharp embedded pebble, and once to remove a piece of dried South Texas wild grass.

She got back in the car, finally.

He put the car into gear and carefully got back on the road after checking for oncoming vehicles.

Right as he reached the speed limit and clicked on the cruise
control, she flung the box of wipes at him. It hit his ear so hard he
lost control of his senses and of the car, and swerved into oncoming traffic. The honk and flashing headlights of a giant eighteen-
wheeler up the road brought him to, and he regained control of the
car and drove back into the northbound lane.

His ear smarted, pulsed red.

She stared into the side-view mirror. Every time the light of the
tower came around, she imagined the puddle of urine glimmering
behind them like a mirage on a fiery South Texas summer day.

He stared directly ahead, pain still pounding.

She peeled another candy bar, popped it whole into her mouth.
When she opened the glove compartment to trash the wrapper,
the air turned sweet again.

At the end of the mile of electric fencing, he saw another sign
warning travelers not to pick up hitchhikers. The prison's spinning
light flashed hypnotically—faintly now—in the rearview mirror.

WHALE ROT

(OR, THE WHALE THAT STUNK UP THE WHOLE TOWN)

What they really wanted to see was the whale's four-foot penis. William the Whale, packed in an old cold-storage transfer trailer—lengthwise—into three-quarters of an eighteen-wheeler parked at the Walmart right off I-35 by the Bordertown Drive-In, by the A&W, by the Cinema I & II. They'd known each other since first grade. Now they were ninth graders, freshmen, finally. Not boyfriend and girlfriend, but BFFs—Diana and Carlitos—BFFs and only that.

Humberto, the skinny, blond-haired, cat-eyed kid from the Mexican side who'd been in school with them since seventh grade, had gone to see the whale with his mom and dad the day before, and he'd told them about it in the hall between first and second period. Said his dad had yelled, "La verga!" when he saw it.

"My mom had to leave the truck she was so embarrassed at my dad," he said.

So the next day, the two of them skipped fourth and fifth period and drove to see the whale in Carlitos's dad's car—a beat-up old Lincoln Continental they thought was luxurious because they could control the gas pedal and the radio's volume with buttons on the steering wheel. Diana particularly liked the shoe box–sized ashtray that pulled out of the dash; she thought it was "super luxurious." Once, when they'd given him a ride from school to the bridge, their friend Alejandro from the Mexican side said to them, "Fucking lazy gringos. Too much trouble to press the fucking gas pedal?"

They drove into the parking lot and saw the trailer right away. There was a giant whale drawn alongside it in what looked like house paints. The painted whale spouted white frothy water as it swam freely in a baby-blue ocean.

They got in line, and it wasn't long before they walked through the rubber-lined metal door atop the squeaky, shaky stairs.

Inside the trailer it was cold, rigged like a giant icebox to help the dead whale keep better in the dirty, thick, yellow formaldehyde it floated in. It was dark in there, too, yet through the darkness, they could see about a foot of giant sutures of heavy twine along the bottom of the whale's tail, curled up and slightly over so that the poor giant fish could fit. There was an old, frayed rope tied around the small of the whale's tail, securing it to the ceiling of the truck. Behind it, as background for the diorama/aquarium/watery tomb, was another cheesy ocean scene in which other whales spouted happily in the distance. There was a half-wood, half-glass wall between them and the fish. The floor of the narrow corridor was covered in rubber to stop visitors from slipping in the humidity. After they had stood in the hundred-degree weather, their bodies now steamed. They laughed at how hokey it all was.

Then they saw it: the whale's huge penis tucked just under its belly. It had been stuffed with hay or dried grass or something. You could see the filling poke through the lousy sutures at the base.

That was when she pulled the Polaroid out of her purse and snapped the photo. The camera flash made the old man come running from the other end of the truck where he'd been selling tickets. Their friends Josie and Patsy had dared them, bet them twenty bucks and year's subscription to *Vampirella* for the penis picture.

"It is clearly spelled out in English on the door as you walk in—N-O-P-I-C-T-U-R-E-S," the old man spelled out. "Can't you frickin' Mexicans read English?" He came at them. "Gimme that picture."

They reacted immediately, pushing past the old man and out the door. The old man almost slipped as he grabbed for them. "Yeah, go on ahead and get the hell outta here, you fucking little wetbacks."

They laughed all the way to the car, parked way out in the middle of the blazing-hot parking lot. They got in the car and drove back toward the old man and shot him the finger as they honked the horn. They could hear him yelling, "I'm gonna call the cops!"

~

They made the kids at school pay anywhere between twenty-five and fifty cents, depending on how "nice" they'd been to them throughout the years, to see the picture of the whale's four-foot penis. They made so much money, they each bought a bag of Cheetos—to which they liked to add Louisiana Hot Sauce—from the candy lady at school for almost two months after that.

~

The day after Diana and Carlitos saw the whale, the truck's cooling system broke down, and the old man had to get a cab and go to both of the two 7-Elevens and to the three supermarkets in town to purchase $2.99 bags of ice.

The disaster made the ten o'clock news: "Several hundred high schoolers, as well as many grown residents of our fair city, have taken advantage of this opportunity to view a specimen of the largest animal God ever created," said Victor Landa. "Keep your fingers crossed that the evening cools off for the whale's sake. . . .

"An expert truck refrigeration mechanic has been called in from Houston, but if there are any mechanics out there who have experience with tractor-trailer refrigeration, please contact us here at the station so that we can get you in touch with Willy the Whale's promoters . . . What? . . . Yes? . . . Oh, sorry, the producer has just informed me that it's William the Whale. Sorry. William the Whale"—and he chuckled—"In the meantime, the show is on hold while the whale has been put on ice . . . if ya know what I mean"—he chuckled again—"until tomorrow. This is Victor Landa, *KRIO News at Ten*. Have a very pleasant evening."

But by early morning the following day, the ice had melted. The temperature never dipped below ninety-three degrees that evening, and the heated metal turned the trailer into a formaldehyde steam bath.

The old man ran around town in a taxi again and got more bags of ice and packed the whale down by late morning. The mechanic was on his way from Houston, he'd been told, but he wouldn't get there for two more days because he'd have to come on his day off—couldn't just up and leave his job.

So the following morning, when the old man opened the two huge metal doors, he saw the whale had exploded, and it poured out of the truck onto the parking lot. A few cars parked right next to the trailer, and even some of the people who, attracted by the news, had come early to see if they could get a peek at the whale, were splattered with stinking, oily, cloudy and putrid, yellow liquid and hardened chunks of organs.

The rubberneckers on the interstate stopped traffic for hours; some even parked on the overpass to watch the city workers clean up the entrails. Those who drove to the Walmart and dared get closer for a look pulled back into their cars and rolled up their windows when they got a whiff of the rotting whale.

One of those spectators appeared on the *Border News at Noon*, head hinged halfway out of his car window to get close to the reporter's microphone, and said, "It smelled like skunk . . . but worse."

By the time the news was on, the old man and his empty fish tank on wheels was driving I-35 headed toward the I-10 junction back to Florida to get another fish. A Greyhound bus sped by. Inside, in the comfort of the air-conditioned coach, sat the mechanic who was supposed to fix the truck, eating a chicken salad sandwich purchased from a woman who got on the bus at Dilley with a basket of goodies to sell.

The eighteen-wheeler dripped a trail of whale juice that evaporated almost as soon as it hit the pavement.

MICROWAVE OVEN

Manolo Ortiz, fourteen years old, craved a snack one Saturday afternoon and burned a bag of popcorn so badly that it caught fire and charred the inside of the microwave oven beyond repair. So he waited at the stop, way out there, the last one on Zapata Highway southeast of the city, for the bus to take him to the only Walmart out on I-35 so he could replace the micro before his mom got home from work that evening. He'd saved enough money from helping his Uncle Ralph sweep up hair at the barbershop on weekends. He had to get it, and he had to do it before eleven o'clock when his mom got home from working all day. He couldn't disappoint her.

It was high noon. The landscape was desolate and dry. The day was bright hot, with not a green thing around except for a giant mesquite tree that lived on what little moisture there might be in the air, and it provided almost no shade with its tiny green leaves.

He waited at the corner for more than twenty-five minutes for the damn bus while the asphalt softened under his feet. Finally, the bus appeared way at the end of as far as his eyes could see. First a dot on the hot horizon, where sky and bush and highway blur, then a blue and white and glassy shine, then a bus at his feet, brakes screeching to a halt. The door opened, and the smell of bus burst cool from inside.

He stepped in. The bus driver quickly shut the bus door behind him and stepped on the gas in order to make the changing traffic light. Manolo leapt forward and grabbed on to the rail so he wouldn't fall. The driver slowed down after speeding across and looked at Manolo and said, "Sorry about that. I'm running late, and the inspectors are being real dogs about sticking to the schedule lately. Sorry."

Manolo was dazed from standing bareheaded in the hot sun for so long. Now securely gripping the bar, he turned, walked slowly down the aisle, and sat down in the almost-empty bus, a couple of seats behind the driver. He took a deep breath of the cool air and settled in for the long ride.

As he sat down, he noticed a large, really overweight woman in tight khaki shorts, sweating, seated at the very front of the bus in one of the seats that faced each other, put in for the elderly and the handicapped. The woman held a giant, bright pink plastic cup filled with ice water between her legs. Manolo was not sure whether the wet spot he noticed between her legs was from condensation around the cup or from her sweat, and he shivered. He was embarrassed that he stared, afraid she might catch him looking, but he couldn't help it—he was fourteen. The cup teeter-tottered on the edge of the seat as she nodded off to sleep then woke frightened, flustered, every time the bus hit a bump. Nonetheless, she always caught the cup just as it was about to slip off the edge of the seat and splash onto the dirty floor.

In the opposite seats, in front of her and behind the driver, sat an old man. His eyes were closed too, and his wrinkled hands were folded gently on top of the curved handle of his cane, and on his dark brown hands, he rested his chin. The old man swayed from side to side every time the driver stepped on the brakes.

The air-conditioning finally cooled Manolo. He started breathing deeply and slowly, and he, too, closed his eyes, relieved of the intense heat. But after a few minutes, he was startled from his rest by the tap, tap, tap of a quarter striking against the glass door of the bus.

He heard the driver murmur something just under his breath, and he didn't pull the lever to open the door.

Three young men in jeans and T-shirts waited at the corner, right next to the bus, tapping on the door to get the driver's attention. The driver just stared ahead, ignoring them. Then the three young men, realizing they would be ignored, crazed from waiting in the heat, began banging on the door with their fists. They knew it would be a long, long and hot time before another bus passed by.

"Get your filthy, cotton-picking hands off my bus, you goddamn wetbacks," he said, finally turning to look straight at them. They were really worked up by now; one even kicked the door, to no avail. The driver just gawked at them. They pounded the door even harder. The one in front yelled obscenities, and spit from his angry mouth sprinkled the glass of the door.

The light turned green.

The driver stepped on the gas and laughed.

What the fuck just happened? Manolo thought.

Suddenly, a blast of noise and glass and burning air exploded from behind. The driver slammed on the brakes, dumbfounded, scared. The fat lady cried out a shrill and piercing yell, shocked and stunned from her sleep by the din of the shattering glass and the freezing water pouring from the cup all over her bare, goosepimpled legs. The old man bellowed an ancient, low, slow groan from somewhere deep inside him. His hands had slipped. His chin had hit the wooden handle of his cane, and he had bitten down hard on his tongue. Blood spurted from his mouth, wide open, and mixed with the ice water all over the rubber-covered floor.

A brick had landed at Manolo's feet with a loud thud. He ducked behind the seat, afraid more stones would come. In the bus's big rearview mirror, he saw them running away from the highway.

Manolo got up slowly, walked to the front of the bus, looked back at the broken window and the three men running, heads disappearing over the shoulder of the road far away. He handed the old man the handkerchief from his back pocket, then yelled at the driver, "Open the fucking door!"

The driver opened the door immediately—only because he was scared shitless—and Manolo stepped quickly off the bus.

He ran. Ran for blocks. Didn't look back. Just kept running. Didn't slow down once. Didn't even stop at the corners and wait for the light to change when he ran across the streets. Just kept running. Right through the Sigmor gas station. Heat rose from the soft pavement in psychedelic blues and greens, mixing with gasoline vapors. He could smell it. He ran down the three long blocks of the street that ran right through the cemetery. Then back up the hill, past the huge cement water tank. Crazed. He ran until he couldn't take another step. He finally dropped down under an orange tree in someone's front yard, unable to catch his breath.

SPLINTER IN THE GUT

Miguel "Cabeza de Pollo" Sanchez got up early that morning and made his way to pick up the forty or so copies of the *Laredo Morning Times*, then to the entrance of the on-ramp of the highway where he sold them. It was literally the first entrance onto the very end of the interstate, or the very beginning, depending on whether you were coming or going, and two traffic signals from the Juárez–Lincoln International Bridge, 1,565 miles from Duluth, Minnesota, the end of the road. He felt weak that morning—standing day after day, year after year, under that brutal South Texas sun was finally all beginning to catch up with him. And on top of that, he'd had a wooden splinter stuck in his belly for three days, and it was now infected.

He was born pigeon-toed and "slow," and his shunned single mother hadn't had the money or the wherewithal to get him the medical care he needed a couple of years after birth when he tried to take his first few steps. So all his life he walked like a chicken, and his oversized nose just added to the avian look. His schoolmates never relented. He dropped out of eighth grade in the middle of his second go at it when, after a history lesson taught by a coach, the other boys turned "Cabeza de Vaca" into "Cabeza de Pollo." He just couldn't take any more. Even now, thirty-something years later, teenagers would sometimes drive by him and cluck.

Three long, hot days before, after a cool shower, he stood in front of the mirror in the tiny bathroom of his tiny apartment, picking at the wooden splinter in his belly with a needle he sterilized black with a match. He could barely see a little bit of brown, he thought, way down under his skin.

"I almost died. Fuck, I almost died!"

He pried and pinched and pushed at the skin around what he was sure was the splinter—but nothing, and he gave up.

"El Pollo" swung the medicine-cabinet mirror open and reached for the bottle of hydrogen peroxide. He tugged off some toilet paper, soaked it in peroxide, and pressed it to his stomach. He cleaned his wound, a tiny pinprick, carefully—it hurt and began to bruise. Finally, as if to make sure all was treated, he stuck the toilet paper into his belly button then went to bed.

As he rolled over to grab a pillow to his chest, he felt a sharp pain in his stomach. He just couldn't sleep. Uncomfortable, he lay there as stiffly as possible until he finally dozed off.

～

This is how he got the splinter in his stomach: He choked on a piece of steak during dinner, and after shoving a finger down his throat did not dislodge the meat, he gave himself the Heimlich by jamming his stomach into the corner of small dinner table he'd inherited long ago when his mother died. This he had learned from his last PE class. Adrenaline had so hyped him up, he hit the corner hard enough to send the chunk—*splat*—onto the linoleum floor on the other side of the table. So hard, the withered wood of the table splintered deep into his belly. Almost immediately, he vomited all over himself.

~

He spent those hours of the morning, that third day after he almost choked to death, hobbling up and down the median until the pain in his belly got so bad that he gave in and weighted the last three copies of the *Laredo Morning Times* with a piece of broken concrete from the crumbling curb and headed downtown to the drugstore for Neosporin.

He walked about five blocks and was already dripping with perspiration—101 degrees at eleven o'clock in the morning.

The hot asphalt opened up in wounds, he thought, cracks that oozed little streams of tar blood when the morning buses and the eighteen-wheelers headed for Mexico rolled heavily over them. The hot breeze the vehicles whooshed cooled his skin when they passed by. As he turned the corner at Salinas and Grant, something fluttered on the ground a few feet ahead of him; in the noon sun, it blazed pearlescent. He was astounded as he drew closer and squatted to the ground, careful not to fall over his feet. A hummingbird, fluttering iridescent green and red and black feathers, had the tip of its long, thin tongue stuck to a piece of red hard candy that was melting on the hot sidewalk.

He almost lost his balance, nervous, one hand on the hot sidewalk, burning him, the other nudging gently under the hummingbird's tiny, thin tongue.

It gave.

The bird lay on the pavement, lifeless, the glow gone from the now-still wings. Then, suddenly, it flew away.

Miguel stared at the glossy piece of hard candy. It melted slowly, but he could see the sweet red liquid flowing from it like a stream; he smelled the sweetness from its release.

He got up, a bit dazed, and made his way to the drug store, got the Neosporin, and slowly walked back home.

⌇

That evening, Miguel "Cabeza de Pollo" Sanchez sat in his living/dining room, staring at the TV until around midnight, when he pushed off the love seat and walked to the bathroom to clean out his wound again. He flicked the light switch on and stood in front of the mirror. He pulled up his T-shirt and bit down to hold it. From the medicine cabinet, he took a bottle of alcohol and a couple of Q-tips. The place where the splinter had entered was tight and red. He pushed the Q-tip deep into his belly button, twirling it slowly. He then squeezed some Neosporin onto the other end of the swab and did the same. It hurt something awful now.

⌇

That night, two mangy dogs fought outside his garage apartment, out in the street by the trash cans. He stared at them from his home's only window. The heat had subsided. A breeze floated through the window—warm, but at least a breeze. Midnight temperature in the midnineties. He stared at the clear South Texas sky, star to star, and then back at the dogs, no longer fighting, each with its piece of whatever they had scavenged.

He saw what was left of the morning glories his mother had planted creep through the torn screen, and this seemed to soothe him.

He slept well later that night, better than he thought he'd be able to. Truth was, he was exhausted.

When he sat up the next morning and inspected his belly, a bump with a ball of pus, like a large pimple, had appeared.

He dressed to go to the other side, the Mexican side, to buy penicillin.

The pharmacy on the Mexican side was way past the mercado. He got the antibiotics easily. They were on sale, stacked on a shelf, self-serve, but he'd have to ask the pharmacist for the pain-killers that he sometimes used when the throbbing in his feet became unbearable.

Miguel paid for the meds and stuck the two boxes into his back pocket and covered them with his shirttails.

On his way back to the bridge, he stopped to buy some candied pumpkin, and the vendor reached for the candy under the glass-top case with a metal tong. Miguel was now sweating heavily. The vendor placed the candy on a piece of wax paper. That's when Miguel noticed the man had no right hand; it had been cut off a few inches above the wrist. The skin looked as if it had been knotted at the end like a balloon. The vendor reached for a small brown paper bag, snapped it open, and held it against his body with his stub. With the other hand, he slipped the candy in. Miguel saw that the candy touched, just barely, the dark hair at the end of the stub, and it made his stomach turn. He paid the vendor and took the candy even though he knew he'd never eat it.

At the bridge, the agents usually just waved pedestrians by after asking about their citizenship and about what they brought back. He stopped midbridge and looked east, the direction the river flowed, imagined it emptying into the Gulf, no idea why he did this in the unbearable heat and with the unbearable pain in his stomach, but he did.

When he got to the American side, he walked up the short set of stairs to the air-conditioned hallway that led to the inspection area. He limped slowly toward the uniformed officer at the end of the hall, past offices on one side, and past glass panels facing the huge covered area where cars are inspected. He said, "Candy," when the man in blue asked, "What are you bringing back?" He thought about declaring the penicillin so the inspector wouldn't question he was bringing anything else (like the banned pain-killers), but decided against it. People crossed with small amounts of illicits all the time. He knew it; everyone did. He flashed open the candy and stated his citizenship, and the inspector waved him on his way. He had walked a few feet when he heard someone yelling, "Sir! Sir!"

He had no idea the official was yelling at him.

Then he felt a firm hand on his shoulder. "Excuse me, sir, but what do you have in your back pocket?"

Fuck! he thought. *Fuck!*

He reached behind him and realized that his shirttail was caught on one of the boxes of medicine, now in plain sight.

"Fuck."

He pulled out the two boxes and handed them to the inspector.

The inspector took a quick look at the boxes and said, "Please come with me, sir."

They walked to the main offices. There were people every-where: Some lined up to apply for temporary visas, some waited for the results of their applications. A child cried as her mother lowered her from the water fountain after a drink. The water had splashed in her nostrils; she had swallowed through her nose. Seated in the very first row of the plastic chairs bolted to the floor, a family shared a roasted chicken. The father tore open the plastic bag of a loaf of sliced bread, then twisted the top off a jar of mayonnaise. Miguel saw the father reach for the chicken, pull a chunk of breast meat off with his fingers, fold it into a slice of soft white bread, and hand it to his boy. The boy sipped on a can of Coke through a straw and reached for the sandwich.

Miguel, now shaking with fear, followed the official into a small room, like a doctor's office. Another inspector joined them. They closed the door. He knew what would come next, so he turned around and, in one quick motion, undid his belt, unbuttoned his jeans, and pulled them down to his knees.

"Wait, wait, wait a minute, sir," said the same inspector who had busted him.

"What are you doing?" asked the other.

"Don't you want me to strip?"

"No, sir, please, pull your pants up," said one of the inspectors.

Miguel did as he was told, and when he tightened his belt, he felt a sharp pain in his stomach again.

The younger of the two inspectors spoke: "One of the medications you had there in your back pocket, the hydrocodone, is a controlled substance. We now have to ask you if we can search your body, but just pat you down, not strip search you, okay?"

He nodded.

"Do you have anything else on you?" the inspector asked. "Is there anything else concealed on your body that you would like to declare?"

"No. . . . What do you want me to do?"

"Just turn around and put your hands on the back of your head," the inspector answered.

One of the men ran his hands down between his legs, all the way down to his boots. He searched inside the boots by pressing with his fingers, paying particular attention to the area around his ankles. As the inspector pressed around his bad feet, Miguel said, "Born that way."

The inspector then asked, "Is there anything sharp inside your pockets or anything I might prick myself with, like a needle or a knife or anything?"

"No."

"Are you sure?" he asked again. "I don't want to put my hand in your pocket and prick myself with an infected needle. I'm gonna be very upset if that happens to me."

"It won't."

The inspector put on Kevlar gloves, just in case, and reached into Miguel's back pocket first and pulled out his wallet. He handed it over to the young inspector, who immediately started searching through it, taking everything out: Miguel's State of Texas ID card—no driver's license, since he'd never been able to drive a car—the picture of his dead mother, and the few dollar bills he'd made that day.

The inspector then asked him to turn around, and he reached into Miguel's pockets and pulled out his house keys on a ring and the Mexican bills and coins that the woman at the pharmacy had given him in change. The inspector placed all of this on a small, wheeled, stainless steel table by the door.

"Okay," he said, "nothing more on him. He's clean."

"I told you."

"Yes," said the inspector, "you did say that."

"Now, Mr. Sanchez," said the other inspector as he read the name on the ID, "we have to go and run this through the system. Please sit down in that chair and wait for us." He pointed at the chair. "Inspector Greene will be standing outside the door until I come back, then we'll both come back to talk to you."

"Please, sir, please, I've never done anything like this before. I usually take the pain-killers for my feet, but now I needed them and some penicillin for this."

He pulled up his shirt and showed the men his infected belly button.

They both cringed.

"Ooh," said the younger, "you should let a doctor see that."

"What the hell do you think I'm going to do with the penicillin—smoke it?" He was angry, and this was not the time for it.

"Hey, hey, Mr. Sanchez," chimed in the older, "be cooperative, and I'm sure we can clear this up. Let us check out your ID, and we'll be right back. Calm down and bite that smart-ass tongue of yours. Okay?"

"Okay."

Miguel waited.

Finally, someone pushed the door open. The inspector handed him his driver's license and a thick yellow slip of paper. He said, "It's a ticket, Mr. Sanchez."

"A ticket? You guys give tickets?"

The inspector looked at him angrily and said, "You prefer to spend the night in a cell? It's a ticket for possession of a controlled substance, the hydrocodone—not the penicillin. Send a check or money order in the envelope. It's like a speeding ticket. Would you prefer us to book you for trying to smuggle drugs into the country?"

"No, sir. No, sir. Not at all, boss."

"Okay, Mr. Sanchez, you can go. Don't do it again," he said. "Ever."

The other inspector smiled at him as he walked out the door. "Don't do it again. Second time, you see the judge . . . and see a doctor about that," he said pointing at Miguel's belly. The inspector then extended his hand for shaking. Miguel gripped it hard and smiled back. He didn't know why, but he was even more nervous now.

A ticket. He couldn't believe it—a ticket!

He walked out of the offices and down the hall as fast as he could, thinking that everyone stared at him through the long wall of glass. He was almost sure he heard those on the other side cackling.

The sore hurt more as he walked. He raised his shirt and looked. The left side of his stomach around his belly button was red-tight and swollen. The ball of pus had flattened out and was no longer white, but a light brown, yellow-pink gel. The swelling was hard to the touch and hurt terribly. His belly button had closed up. He poked his little finger inside as best he could but didn't get in too far, pulled it right back out, it was so painful—a quick, sharp pain stabbed immediately, then came a dull, throbbing pain.

He smelled his pinky. It stank.

He rotted inside.

Miguel walked home slowly in the scorching air.

⌒

After he got home, Miguel slept all afternoon from outright fatigue. The familiar music of the six o'clock news woke him. The Mexican news. The voice warned viewers in Spanish that the scenes would not be suitable for children: Two bodies, bloated, beached, like cattle after a flood, by the river. Their faces TV-blurred. The camera panned a little further down the river. A child's body, bloated too, like the lost fat baby of a giant. TV-blurred too. "This brings the total to two hundred and seven river-related deaths in the Rio Grande this year. We'll be right back after these words from our local sponsor," said the familiar voice.

Miguel had a fever.

Still exhausted, he fell back asleep.

⌒

He woke up maybe an hour later, the pain so great, and made his way to the bathroom like a sleepwalker.

Even in this semiconscious state, he knew he'd have to go back across and get the penicillin again. It wasn't getting any better with the Neosporin alone. The penicillin he could cross without a problem. Too bad the inspectors had confiscated his.

He twisted a couple of squares of toilet paper to a point again and stuck it in his belly button in hopes that the sore would drain. He forced the last button of his jeans closed so that his pants would hold the toilet paper in place.

Once again, he walked out into the heat of the evening, strangely relieved at his decision to walk all that way across town again, across the bridge again, across downtown Nuevo Laredo again, in the searing heat, pigeon-toed, not knowing which hurt more—his poor feet or his belly. He was in a daze.

~

He stood on Convent Street, staring south at the Mexican side for just a little while, huge Mexican flag hanging limp on its pole, cars bumper-to-bumper in both directions, and started walking toward the bridge.

He crossed half the bridge, stopped to rest. Cars honked as if it really made a difference. One had overheated. Bent over under the hood of his car, a man twisted open the radiator cap, a dirty rag in his other hand for protection against the boiling fluid he knew would come. After the wild explosion, its mist fell softly on Miguel's face. People honked incessantly, as if they'd get around the stalled car.

A cloud of black smoke from a muffler not three feet away, followed by hot, putrid river vapors sent Miguel into a coughing fit.

He made his way back to the same pharmacy and again bought

the same meds—both—as easily as he had just earlier that day. *Fuck it*, he thought. He'd chance it again, but this time he carefully pressed each pill through its foil cover and pushed the antibiotics and the pain-killers deep down into the pocket of his jeans.

What are the chances the same inspectors will be there again? he thought. And anyway, at this point he didn't care if they caught him again. *Maybe they'll put me in jail where they'll get me a doctor finally.*

Miguel made his way back to the bridge, nervous. He paid the pedestrian toll, and as he pushed the toll counter down in front of him, he felt his shirt was humid, wet. He pushed through to get away from a small crowd that had gotten onto the bridge right behind him and put his hand to his stomach; something seemed to give. For a split second, his stomach hurt intensely, but the pain subsided almost immediately. He reached down at his sore to feel something hard and foreign. He stopped, pulled up his T-shirt, and saw the dark head of the splinter. He pinched it with his fingers to pull it out, but it slipped—it was coated with pus. So he wiped his fingers on his T-shirt and went at it again. This time, he got a good hold of it with his nails and pulled.

He was amazed, astonished, overwhelmed by the size. It was almost two inches long and thicker than a wooden matchstick. He stared at it in awe for just a second, put it up to his face to look at it more closely after wiping off the smelly pus that coated it on his T-shirt.

He took a long, deep breath of the warm night and placed the splinter into the coin pocket of his jeans carefully so that it wouldn't break. Then he reached into either pocket, grabbed the meds, and dumped them into the gritty giant trash cans glowing orange under the giant halogen lights.

REDHEAD

Her hair caught fire years ago, Christmastime, as she bent over to light a cigarette on the gas stove one night—stinking drunk. It never grew back right after that, patchy and frizzy and uncombable, so she shaved her head with disposable Bic razors in the shower every other morning.

Since she could choose hair color now, she wore a red wig of real human hair she'd found for thirty-five dollars at the Goodwill Store. It had been combed semiprofessionally by women from Goodwill's back-to-work program. When she'd first seen it, she held it up in front of her and scrutinized it carefully, her eyesight already beginning to go from old age, then she slipped it on and stared at herself in the mirror. One of the girls working close to the counter was cleaning out an old chest of drawers someone had donated; she looked at her and said, "That's real nice, ma'am. Real nice."

Two years later, she wore it still, though now it was uncombed and wild, kind of like the fire.

She didn't quit smoking; in fact, she sucked on those cigarettes even more now, had to have one pack within reach, another waiting in the freezer, always. And this was where she was headed determinedly early that morning—to buy cigarettes at the corner store, and a tallboy.

"These damn cigarettes are gonna kill me, Johnny. Don't know why you keep selling 'em to me," she said to the man behind the counter as she popped the beer can open.

He smiled, grinned, then chuckled a bit and pointed to the old, yellowed State of Texas notice tacked to the wall behind him, "Now, Matilde, you know you can't drink that in here." Then he broke into a laugh outright.

That's when she saw herself in the round mirror positioned at an angle above the man's head so he could see behind him when he turned his back.

She had forgotten to put on her wig.

He regained his composure, not sure how she'd react to his laughter. "It's not those cigarettes that are gonna kill you, Matilde." He chuckled. "It's that beer."

"What're you staring at?" she asked gruffly, placing the exact amount she paid every morning—seven wrinkled dollar bills wrapped around forty-seven cents change—on the counter. "You keep staring at me, and I'm gonna cross the interstate and go buy my cigarettes at the Walmart and probably get hit by an eighteen-wheeler while crossing. That'll teach you, make you feel guilty for laughing at a poor, old, bald woman. Huh?" she said and stormed out of the store. An electronic bell chimed behind her.

Two years ago, she turned sixty, then she lost her job, then she was too old to get another. She used up what she'd saved from working for years without benefits at Woolco then at the Walmart that had taken its place—the very same Walmart she threatened to take her business to. They'd always managed to schedule her hours just short of qualifying for benefits. Not much you can save on minimum wage. When she'd finally gone through that in a little over a year, her neighbors—the old woman, Sofia, who lived with her sister, Minerva, down the street; the Saldaña family, who went away half the year to work the canning season in Blue Island near Chicago; and the Rodriguez family, who had welcomed her into the garage apartment they'd fixed up to make some extra money from rent—they had all taken care of her, bringing tacos and egg sandwiches and leftovers and tamales at Christmas until she started drinking and stopped eating much.

"It's curious that she'd start drinking at such an age," Mrs. Rodriguez whispered to her husband. "Especially since she never drank before, you know? She told me she never really cared for the booze." She'd said that one day when they had to help her get into the apartment after Matilde thought she'd misplaced her keys. Turns out the keys were in her bosom, wrapped in some crumpled dollar bills. They fell out when she almost fell over, and Mr. Rodriguez caught her with one hand and the keys with the other.

At sixty-one years of age, Matilde Morton resorted to twirling a baton she'd found outside St. Peter's Memorial School on a night when she'd been so drunk she'd lost her way back from drinking on the Mexican side—it was cheaper there. She did this for about a week—stood on the side of a main road leading to the interstate, far away on the north side of town, two bus transfers from her apartment to make sure no one in her neighborhood knew. She imagined herself back in school, however many years ago it had been, when she'd been a cheerleader in Lytle, Texas, just south of San Antonio. She found she was still really good at it—or so she thought. She rolled her sleeves as far up her arm as possible to throw that baton up into the heavens and attempt to catch it. People honked and whistled and jeered and threw money.

She didn't belong here, here in this sea of Mexican people, where her pink skin now sagged red under each arm as she tossed the baton from one hand to the other. Was she really remembering her youth? Did someone tell her, "Hey, Matilde, if you're gonna make any money here, you need some kind of trick, a show, like the fire-eaters on the Mexican side . . . if you're gonna make it here, you gotta have something good enough to make them roll down their windows in this goddamned heat long enough to toss you a coin . . . you've gotta make it worth the air-conditioning they lose when they do."

But she made almost twenty dollars her first day, and more the second, and the third, and the entire week, until a bus driver friend of Mr. Rodriguez told him he thought he recognized the woman who lived in the garage apartment twirling a baton on the side of the road. They jumped in the car, found her, and forced her in; she was woozy and dehydrated, the dangling flesh of her arms sunburned as red as the wig slightly off to the side of her head.

Mrs. Rodriguez cried.

"Why, honey, what you crying for?" Matilde asked, then closed her eyes and fell asleep in the backseat, red flesh pulsing something awful.

Thank God a month or so later she turned sixty-two and filed for social security. Now she spent most of the time at home drunk, watching TV, except when she took the short walk to the corner grocery store, or when she took the trash out every three or four days, or when she went to the bank downtown to cash her social security check.

And so it had been that day. She went back to her little apartment, adjusted the wig on her head as she looked into the blotchy mirror in the bathroom and cursed Johnny for laughing at her. She walked to her bed and reached between the mattress and box spring for the check, which had come in the mail just yesterday. She folded the check, still in its envelope, and slipped it into the hollow of her bra.

THE BORDER IS BURNING

Everybody sleeps. At some point. Everybody needs to sleep. Gonzalo Gonzalez needed sleep badly. And cash. A lot of it. Around sixteen grand.

As he started getting closer to his neighborhood, he saw a thin plume of smoke on the horizon, white smoke, then gray smoke, then white smoke again, against the dark, almost blue-black sky. The sirens got louder and louder as he got closer and closer to his home. But he knew already. He knew it was his house burning, and he knew who started the fire.

He should've known better, really. But Gonzalo Gonzalez broke the first rule of dealing: don't use.

A couple months back, early evening, he cut two fat lines with his debit card, one for his friend "Weasel" Valdez, and one for himself—two lines that started a weekend binge that he regretted the minute the shit hit the back of his throat. When he realized how much he and Weasel had done, he got so nervous, so obsessed with trying to figure out how he was going to pay *them* back that he kept doing more. Weasel got so scared he split.

His supplier told him to come in but made him sweat it out for three days, three long days before he got the call. Gonzalo only knew the guy as Jerry. And although he'd only been moving coca for them for six, maybe seven months, Jerry told him, "Relax, we'll carry you for a couple weeks," and fronted him more cocaine—a couple thousand dollars' worth—after Gonzalo promised to get it back to them in a week. "You give us all you make—your cut too. Then we'll do it again next week. And we'll keep doing it this way, and if everything goes all right, then you'll be paid up real quick, and you can start making some cash for yourself."

"Nah, man, I'll move it for you. No problem. I promise. You know I'm good. You know I can move this shit," he said, almost crying.

So on his way back home that hot afternoon, right before he got back on I-35, he pulled into La Marquesa Apartments on Gua-temozín Street, drove to the end of a building with a giant #7 painted across a wall of bricks, and reversed his truck into a spot under the shade of a big pecan tree. There, he could see if any-one was coming. He pulled out one of the big plastic bags they'd fronted him, fiddled with the zip seal for what seemed like a long time because he was so drained. He had to have a little, just a lit-tle, after what he'd just been through, after being up and worried for so many days. When he finally got it open, Gonzalo pulled his keys from the ignition, loaded up a big bump, and put the key up to his nose while he looked at himself in the rearview mirror to make sure it was right at the nostril so he wouldn't lose any. Then, almost immediately, he dug back in and took another hit to the other nostril. He calmed down, took a deep breath, felt the back of his throat start to numb up again, then went back in for another round. Just a little more. A little more. Gonzalo then licked the key clean, pushed it back into the ignition, and headed home.

When he got back to his house that afternoon, he called Weasel, who showed up at the front porch within the hour with a couple six-packs and a couple hundred dollars. They promised each other they'd only do two hundred dollars' worth of the stuff. But the binge lasted all weekend, and now he owed them so much money, he knew he could never pay them back.

When he was called in again—no three-day wait this time— "El Crazy" Marinez squeezed his throat tight against the wall. He squeezed so hard, Gonzalo Gonzalez agreed to the deal, to be a mule. Just once, promised Jerry, as he motioned for Marinez to let Gonzalo go. Really simple: go across the bridge, pick up the stuff, walk it back across.

"Easy," he promised. "Just one time."

They asked him his shoe size and what size belt he wore and told him to go home, have a beer, relax, try and get some sleep. But he didn't. Didn't sleep for days. He walked around wound up on adrenaline, his shirts buttoned all the way up to hide the five fat finger marks around his neck.

Marinez showed up unannounced at Gonzalo's house one afternoon a few days later. He whispered an address on the Mexican side into his ear. Explained exactly how to get there: "Not too far off from the mercado, not more than five or six blocks from the bridge, and a few blocks off Guerrero. . . .

"When you get there, just knock; they know who you are. They know you're coming. When you get inside, ask to use the bathroom. They'll take you. Inside the bathroom there's a pair of shoes, your size, and a belt. Take off your shoes and put those on. Take off your belt and put on the one that's there. Walk back across the bridge and then go to San Agustin Plaza, and we'll be there to pick you up."

Gonzalo was really scared. No one went across anymore. It was way too dangerous. No one.

"When do you want me to go?"

"Now," he said. "Go now."

⤳

He did it. Quickly and without incident. In less than two hours, Gonzalo Gonzalez set foot back on American soil late that afternoon. Anxious and nervous and feeling like he wanted to vomit, he steadied himself to cross Grant Street and walked the half a block to the plaza in front of the cathedral. He could see Marinez feeding coins into the parking meter. Gonzalo made his way up to him.

Marinez saw him coming and held open the backseat door of a rusty silver Toyota and pointed him in. He slid across the seat. On the seat, there was a pair of black tennis shoes. As Gonzalo slipped off the loafers he'd found waiting for him in the bathroom across the river, Marinez stuck his head in through the window and whispered, "Don't forget the belt too." After he'd changed shoes, Gonzalo took off the belt, rolled it up tight, and pushed it into one of the loafers. Marinez peeked his head in again and said, "Go home. Get the hell out of here."

Gonzalo attempted to open the door, but El Crazy said, "No, get out on that side, the other side. Look out for the cars when you open the door. Hey, and get some sleep. You look like shit."

⤳

The evening sun had just set. Gonzalo Gonzalez, still several blocks away from his house, felt a burning in his throat, an acrid taste at the base of his tongue, coming up and stinging.

He walked slowly. But he knew already. He knew exactly where the smoke was coming from. He wasn't looking, not really;

he was afraid to look, so he stared directly in front of him, straight ahead into nowhere, into nothing, into the darkness, thick. As he turned the corner, the reflection of a bright orange glow erupted onto the pupils of his dark brown eyes.

The smoke that billowed from his burning house finally hit him, swirled at his nose, down inside each nostril, burned the back of his throat, made him cough.

Then, the flashing red lights brought him to. Cops stood on either side of the blocked-off street. A reporter on the sidewalk stood as close to the burning house as the fire fighters would let him. Neighbors, even some who lived too far away to be real neighbors, huddled, staring at the roaring fire. Gonzalo focused on a woman making the sign of the cross in the orange glow. He glided through the small crowd until a cop yelled at him, "All right, far enough! That's far enough." His neighbor and his neighbor's wife, an elderly couple he'd known all his life, old friends of his parents, whose house he had inherited and now lived in—used to live in—came to comfort him. As if on signal, the reporter rushed over, cameraman running behind him, light man, with battery pack and light, running behind him. The old woman pushed her hand open against the camera lens; her husband barked at the reporter, "Leave him alone. Get the hell outta here," just like he'd heard on the live cop shows on TV. The cameraman pulled away. The reporter repositioned himself to continue taping at a distance. Gonzalo, now as if in a trance, stared directly into the camera.

"We've been told by neighbors that this young man who just arrived at the scene is the owner of the house that has now been almost completely destroyed by the fire."

Suddenly, the flames caused a fire storm of sorts, a wind all its own that made the huge flames spin and churn and suddenly leap out toward the street, like flare-ups on the sun. The fire just barely touched one of the few surviving palm trees that the city had planted on the sidewalk all along the neighborhood many years ago; it caught fire quickly.

The cameraman pointed his camera at the burning palm tree. Somebody gasped. Gonzalo, still in a daze, watched as one of the dried lower palm fronds burned, snapped, then floated off the tree like a falling kite, oscillating all akimbo. The glowing end of the frond lit a red line in the darkness like fluorescent tempera.

The cameraman took two or three quick steps back when he realized that the frond was coming right down at him. But it was too late; the thorns that ran along the palm frond's stem stuck sharply into his flesh. He fell to his knees more in shock than in pain and managed to lay the camera somewhat gently onto the hot, softened blacktop.

Then a loud boom exploded from the Mexican side.

"That was really close!" the reporter yelled.

"Get the first aid kit," the cameraman pleaded.

Seven more thundering blasts, one right after the other, echoed across the river, then flashed like lightning across the sky.

Printed in the USA
CPSIA information can be obtained
at www.ICGtesting.com
CBHW052157190324
5600CB00001B/54

9 780826 365668